从经典作家进入历史

希尼在威克洛郡，一九七一年
（Jack McManus 摄，Co. Wicklow）

希尼出生于北爱尔兰德里郡。他的第一本诗集
《一个博物学家之死》初版于一九六六年，后
又出版了诗歌、批评和翻译作品，使他成为他
那一代诗人中的翘楚。一九九五年，他获得诺
贝尔文学奖；两度荣获惠特布莱德年度图书奖
（《酒精水准仪》，1996；《贝奥武甫》，1999）。
由丹尼斯·奥德里斯科尔主持的访谈录《踏脚
石》出版于二〇〇八年；他的最后一本诗集《人
之链》获得二〇一〇年度前瞻诗歌奖最佳诗集
奖。二〇一三年，希尼去世。他翻译的维吉尔
《埃涅阿斯纪》第六卷在其去世后出版（2016），
赢得批评界盛誉。

◇中英双语版◇

越冬

北方

[爱尔兰] 谢默斯·希尼 著　朱玉 译

广西师范大学出版社
·桂林·

Wintering Out by SEAMUS HEANEY
First published in 1972
North by SEAMUS HEANEY
First published in 1975
This edition arranged with Faber and Faber Ltd. through Big Apple Agency, Inc.,
Labuan, Malaysia
Simplified Chinese edition copyright © 2024 Guangxi Normal University Press Group
Co., Ltd.

著作权合同登记号桂图登字:20 - 2024 - 003 号

图书在版编目(CIP)数据

越冬;北方:汉、英/(爱尔兰)谢默斯·希尼著;朱玉译. —
桂林:广西师范大学出版社,2024.5
(文学纪念碑)
书名原文:Wintering Out/North
ISBN 978 - 7 - 5598 - 6955 - 5

Ⅰ. ①越… Ⅱ. ①谢… ②朱… Ⅲ. ①诗集-爱尔兰-现代-
汉、英 Ⅳ. ①I562.25

中国国家版本馆 CIP 数据核字(2024)第 098064 号

越冬·北方:汉、英
YUEDONG·BEIFANG;HAN,YING

出 品 人:刘广汉　　　策　　划:魏 东　　　责任编辑:魏 东　程卫平
助理编辑:钟雨晴　　　装帧设计:赵 瑾
广西师范大学出版社出版发行

(广西桂林市五里店路9号　　　邮政编码:541004)
(网址:http://www.bbtpress.com)
出版人:黄轩庄
全国新华书店经销
销售热线:021 - 65200318　021 - 31260822 - 898
山东临沂新华印刷物流集团有限责任公司印刷
(临沂高新技术产业开发区新华路1号　邮政编码:276017)
开本:889 mm × 1 194 mm　1/32
印张:10.625　　　字数:318 千
2024 年 5 月第 1 版　2024 年 5 月第 1 次印刷
定价:72.00 元

越　冬

1972

给戴维·哈蒙德和迈克尔·朗利

今天早晨从露湿的高速公路
我看到关押拘留犯的新营地：
一枚炸弹在路边留下一处
新土坑，而那边的树丛里

机枪哨界定真实的防御。
那里有你在低地常见的白雾
而这似曾相识，如讲述十七号
战俘营的电影，一场无声的噩梦。

死之前可有生？这句话被粉笔
写在市中心的墙上。胜任苦痛，
患难与共，一箪食，一瓢饮，
我们再度拥抱卑微的宿命。

目 录

第二部分

致谢与注释

感谢以下书刊的编者，本诗集中的大部分作品曾发表在这些书刊上，其中很多诗在形式上略有不同：

《水瓶座》、《亚特兰蒂斯》、《标准》(戈尔韦)、《批评季刊》、《学士袍》、《卫报》、《海伯尼亚》、《诚实的阿尔斯特人》、《爱尔兰新闻》、《爱尔兰时报》、《倾听者》、《马拉哈特评论》、《密歇根评论季刊》、《新政治家》、《西方》、《凤凰》、《诗歌》(芝加哥)、《诗书学会增刊》、《立场》、《门槛》。

感谢《现代诗人聚焦2》(柯基)和《英国青年诗人选》(查托)的编者。

《炉边》和《夏日之家》第二、五部分(原名《家》和《晨歌》)版权属于《纽约客》，1971年。

《土地》、《男仆》和《夏日之家》第三、四部分曾以宽幅报刊形式由每月诗歌、红发汉拉翰出版社和塔拉电话出版。

《私生子》曾发表在《12/12》(卡姆登诗歌节，1970)；《男仆》发表在《回应》(国家图书联盟与诗歌协会，1971）。

《图伦男子》和《内尔瑟斯》的灵感来自 P.V. 戈劳布的《沼泽人》（费伯）。

"Maighdean Mara"：爱尔兰语，"美人鱼"［第 83 页诗歌标题］。

第一部分

牧 草

或者，我们会说，

*fother*①，我再次

为它张开

双臂。但首先

去拉扯紧紧

盘绕的草垛

饱经风霜的草檐

从草垛上

落在你脚边，

去年夏天翻晒的

一片片青草

和绣线菊

多得如同面包

和鱼，拿起一捆

---

① "牧草"（fodder），在希尼的方言中，发音为"fother"。（本书脚注皆为译者注）

轻轻抛过半门

或丢进肮脏的缝隙。

这些长夜

我将扯干草

以求安慰，任何

能铺好马厩的东西。

沼泽橡

马车夫的战利品
劈成房椽，
布满蛛网、乌黑、
风干已久的拱肋

在第一层茅草下。
我也许可以
和那些大胡子
逝者、背箩筐的人在一起，

或偷偷聆听
他们无望的智慧
当被风吹回的烟
在半门间挣扎

当蒙蒙细雨
模糊了
马车路的尽头。
软软的车辙

不会带你回到
"橡树林"，不会
遇见在绿色空地
剪槲寄生的人。

也许我只认出了
埃德蒙·斯宾塞，
他正梦想着阳光，
被地方的守护神

侵扰，它们蹑手蹑脚
"从树林和山谷的
每一个角落出来"
爬向水田芥和腐尸。

安娜霍里什 [①]

我的"清水之地"，
世上第一座山丘
那里的泉水涌入
闪亮的青草

和小巷路基上
黯淡的卵石。
安娜霍里什，辅音的
缓坡，元音草场，

灯火余影
在冬日黄昏的
院子里摇晃。
带着桶和手推车

那些圆丘的原住民
走入齐腰的迷雾
去井边和粪堆
击碎薄冰。

---

① 安娜霍里什（Anahorish），诗人度过童年并上小学的地方。

男　仆

他正在越冬，
坏年月的年根，
摇晃一盏防风灯
穿过某间茅棚；

影子零工。
老仆人，奴隶
血统，曾登上集市山
在每个出价者的注视下

保持你的耐心
并守口如瓶，你
如何将我拖入
你的足迹。你的足迹

断续，从干草地到马厩，
散落的牧草
在雪地上僵硬，
新年里最先跨过

小男爵的

后门：愤恨

而不悔改，

带来温热的蛋。

最后的伶人

一

揣一枚石子在兜里，
一根桦杖在肘下。

走出草地的
迷雾，蹑脚踏上台阶。

角落里刺眼的电视屏幕
让人们着迷围成一圈

于是他在他们身后站了许久。
圣乔治、别西卜和草杰克

无法从迷雾中召来。
他的拳头握紧手杖

并且，假扮下，开始
击打门栏。

他的靴子踏裂马路。石子

从石瓦上噼啪坠落。

二

他从乡村
禁忌的束缚中走来

择一条好路穿过
流血与世仇的

漫长征途。
他的舌在文明的舌间

做着无谓的事情，
他有着善察阴晴的眼睛

在十字路口或小巷尽头
能根据窗帘的颤动

做出各种伪装。
他绝妙的草面具和佝偻背

消失在灯火点亮的
院落石板外。

三

你梦见壁炉里有蟋蟀
地板上有蟑螂，

一队伶人
齐步走出房门

灯盏在寒风中闪烁。
他们脚下的融雪

让你平静。
又一旧年逝于

你的炉石之上，祝好运。
月亮的圣体升起

在冬青树的圣体匣，
他辟出幽暗的小路，亦曾

清扫最初的露湿小径
通往夏日的草场。

土　地

一

我步测它，一杆又一杆①。

解开缠绕的灯芯草和青草

开启我的通行权

穿过旧低洼和播种地

从耕地旁捡起石子

立起小小的石堆。

清理水渠，修剪树篱

常常破晓起床

漫步边远的田野。

我为那几亩田养成这些习惯

以便我最后的目光

不贪婪也不饥饿。

我随时准备去任何地方。

---

① 杆（perch）：从九世纪开始在英语世界沿用至今的长度单位，通常用于测量土地，一杆大约五米。

二

这可以代替我的遗迹
收割后的长坡上
梳着辫子，枝蔓丛生：

一个湿腐叶做的女人，
灯芯草作饰带，茅草作饰边，
松散地堆立着，她镂空的乳房

用新稻草和丰收结做成。
目光掠过
奔跑的野兔。

三

我感到爪垫
在青草和三叶草下展开：

如果我躺下
让耳朵在这寂静圈

够久，股骨
和肩膀贴紧这幻影的地面，

我想我会接收到
一阵轻微的鼓声

且一定不会吃惊
若在爆破的空气里

发现自己陷入圈套，摇晃
一只尖铁丝做的耳环。

雨的礼物

一

骤雨和持续的滂沱如今
已有数日。

　　　　　安静的哺乳动物，
在淤泥上脚跟未稳，
开始用他的皮肤
感知天气。

洪水敏捷的口鼻
舔舐一块块踏脚石
连根拔起一切。
　　　　　　他涉过
他的生命，凭借测听。
　　　　　　　　测听。

二

一个男人涉过失落的田野
打破洪水的窗玻璃：

一枝泥浆的花朵
向着他的倒影绽开

像一道伤口
在水盆里摇曳它的红印。

他的双手搜寻
铁锹掀翻的

沉陷的田垄，他所依靠的
亚特兰蒂斯。于是

他被紧箍在他耕耘的地方
天空和土地

在他摸索农田的
双臂间自然流淌。

三

当雨水积聚
浅滩就会
彻夜轰鸣。
他们被尘世调教的耳朵

能监听寻常的

万物齐语，急流

在山墙边喋喋不休，

默尤拉①在砾石河床

奏响竖琴：

天亮时所有漩流

都涨满各自的曲调

并溢出每一只水桶

如长长的发缕。

我侧耳倾听

一个缺席——

在血脉的共同召唤中

我感到急需

大洪水之前的知识。

逝者轻柔的声音

正在岸边低语

我想要打探

---

① 希尼童年时家乡的河。

（为了我的孩子们）

为何庄稼腐烂，河泥

釉涂烤熟的泥床。

四

茶色的喉音的河水

拼写它自己：默尤拉

是它自身的总谱和乐队，

使地方安眠于

它的语声，

芦笛的音乐，古老的笛管

轻吐它的雾气

吹过元音和历史。

涨满的河流，

求偶的声音

涌起取悦我，富人，

共同土地的守护者。

图　姆^①

我的嘴撑圆
轻柔的爆破音，
图姆，图姆，
仿佛在舌头

错位的石板下
闯入一间地下室
在一万年间的
肥土、燧石、火枪弹、

破碎的陶片、
铁项圈和鱼骨针里
勘探有什么新物件
直到我被卷入

沼泽水和支流下
突然倾覆的
冲积淤泥，
幼鳗缠绕我的头发。

_____
① 图姆（Toome），离诗人童年的家只有一步之遥的村庄。

布罗赫①

河岸，长长的犁沟
止于阔叶酸模
一条林荫道
直达浅滩。

花园里的霉菌
很容易碰伤，阵雨
积聚在你的足印
是布罗赫

黑色的 O，
它低沉的鼓点
在多风的接骨木
和大黄叶片间

几乎戛然
而止，像最后的
gh，异乡人总是
难以掌握。

---

① 布罗赫，原文是 Broagh，盖尔语"河岸"的意思，位于诗人家
乡默尤拉河岸附近。

神 谕

藏在一棵柳树的

空树干里，

它聆听熟悉的声音，

直到，一如既往，他们

在田间重复呼喊

你的名字。

你能听见他们

拉开栅栏门，

当他们接近

唤你出来：

树洞里的

小嘴和耳朵，

苔藓地带的

耳垂与喉。

后　视

空中的摇晃

仿佛语言的

失效，翅膀的

伎俩。

沙锥鸟的咩咩声逃离

它的筑巢地

逃入方言，

逃入变体，

音译嗡鸣

在自然保护区上空——

空中的小山羊，

夜晚的小山羊，

凌霜的小山羊。①

---

① 盖尔语中对"沙锥鸟"的民间称呼有多种，比如"gabhairín
reo"，意为"凌霜的小山羊"；"gabhar reo"，意为"凌霜的山
羊"；"gabhar oíche"，意为"夜晚的小山羊"；等等。山羊与沙
锥鸟的关联由此可见。

是它的尾羽

在大雁和

黄色麻鳽的

滑流中

击响挽歌

当它盘旋飞离

飞入我们

赖以生存的地窖，飞过

狙击手①的秘巢，

飞过暮光中的堡垒

和墙垣，

消失于

田野工作者

梳理归档的

采集物和残余物。

---

① 狙击手（sniper）与沙锥鸟（snipe）拼写相似。

传　统

给汤姆·弗兰纳根[①]

一

我们喉音的缪斯
很久以前遭到
头韵传统的凌辱，
她的小舌退化

萎缩，被忘却
仿佛尾骨
或布里吉德十字
枯黄在某间茅屋

而习俗，那位
"至高无上的女主人"，
让我们寄宿在
不列颠的岛屿。

---

① 即托马斯·弗兰纳根（Thomas Flanagan，1923–2002），加州
大学伯克利分校教授、小说家，擅长爱尔兰文学研究，著有
《爱尔兰小说家 1800–1850》（1958）。

二

我们将自豪地说
我们的伊丽莎白式英语：
"大学"①，比如说，
是我们草根的用词；

我们"认为"②或我们"准许"③
当我们猜想
而一些珍爱的古语
是无误的莎士比亚风。

更不用说那低地人
卷舌的辅音
固执地穿梭于
防御墙和苔藓地。

---

① varsity,（英、旧）大学。在英国，只有极少数人使用该词。
② deem,（正式）认为。
③ allow, 准许。

三

麦克莫里斯①，游荡

在环球剧院，向着

廷臣和观众抱怨

他们听说我们

落后不堪，缺乏

教养，就像野兔，

像死亡的躯壳：

"我的民族是什么？"

然后明智地，尽管来得

太迟了，流浪的布鲁姆

答道："爱尔兰，"布鲁姆说，

"我出生于此。爱尔兰。"

---

① 莎士比亚《亨利五世》中的爱尔兰士兵。

新　曲

我遇见一个女孩，来自德里加夫①
这名字，一种遗失的雄烈麝香，
让人想起河流蜿蜒之处，
黄昏时翠鸟如蓝箭弩张

踏脚石就像乌黑的磨牙
陷入浅滩，水上的旋涡
变幻着釉彩，默尤拉
在赤杨树下尽情快活。

而德里加夫，我想，只是，
消失的音乐，暮光下的水，
敬给过去的玉液琼汁
被这偶遇的处子祭酹。

但此刻我们的河流之舌必须涨潮
必须从深深舐舐的故地涌起

---

① 一个小村庄，离希尼小时候住的地方很近。下文卡索道森和
阿珀兰兹也是。

成为洪水，用元音的拥抱，
淹没辅音分界的领地。

我们还要征募卡索道森
和阿珀兰兹，每一个城池——
像青草延续洗晒的绿茵——
一个语音，如史前要塞和祭石。

另一边

一

在深及大腿的莎草和金盏花里
一个邻居把他的影子投在
小溪，断言

"像拉撒路一样贫瘠，那片地"，
然后沙沙走过
摇摇晃晃的枝叶：

我躺在他的草坡
与我们的休耕地相接的地方，
安卧在苔藓和灯芯草上，

我的耳朵吞下
他自命不凡的圣经式不屑，
上帝选民的语气。

当他像那样站在
另一边，白发苍苍，
挥舞他的黑刺李手杖

指点沼泽的野草，

他在我们贫瘠的田地上预言，

然后转身离去

走向他在山上的

应许之地，一缕花粉

飘向我们这边，下一季的稗子。

二

连续数日我们背诵

每一位族长的箴言：

拉撒路，法老，所罗门

还有大卫和歌利亚

盛大涌来，像满载的干草

超过我们小巷的负荷，

或在车辙上蹒跚——

"你们那一边，我以为，

几乎完全不遵守圣经。"

他的大脑是刷白的厨房

挂满经文，打扫干净
如同教堂中厅。

三

然后有时当玫瑰经哀婉地
在厨房里拖延
我们会听见他的脚步来到山墙边

尽管直到连祷文结束
外面才会传来敲门声
悠闲的口哨才会在

门阶响起。"今晚天气不错，"
他会说，"我闲逛路过，
心想，不妨来串个门。"

但此刻我站在他身后
在幽暗的院子里，在祈祷的呻吟里。
他把一只手放进衣兜

或害羞地用黑刺李手杖轻轻敲出
一段小曲，仿佛他撞见了
恋人在亲昵或陌生人的啜泣。

我该溜走吗，我想，

还是上前拍拍他的肩膀

跟他聊聊天气

或草籽的价格？

羊毛贸易

"羊毛贸易"——闲谈中
他说起这词语，如温暖的羊毛

飘出他的秘藏。
剪毛，捆扎、漂洗、梳理

从他元音的线轴上
松解开来

罩衣下魁梧的人们
谈天中堆积轻柔的地名

比如布鲁日，比如
从尼德兰返回的商贾：

哦，所有的小村庄

044

那里的山峦、羊群和溪流

合谋一种水车的语言，
织机与纺锤的遗失句法，

它们如何挂在
那儿褪色，在语言的画廊！

而我必须说起粗花呢，
一种僵硬的布料，斑驳如血。

亚麻城

主街，贝尔法斯特，一七八六年①

现在是三点四十
公共时钟显示。穿斗篷的骑手
哒哒走进画面

也许来自亚麻厅②
也许是谷物集市
在那里，市政画解冻，

十二年后
他们绞死年轻的麦克拉肯③——
穿低领衫的美女和戴三角帽的少爷

---

① 一七八六年市政部门印刷的一幅钢笔水彩画。画中呈现了亚麻集市和谷物集市。

② 亚麻厅（Linen Hall），位于贝尔法斯特多尼戈尔广场北 17 号，原为集市，一七八八年成为图书馆，是贝尔法斯特最古老的图书馆。

③ 亨利·乔伊·麦克拉肯（Henry Joy McCracken，1767-1798），生于贝尔法斯特一个富裕的亚麻商家庭。领导联合爱尔兰人协会发起一七九八年起义，反对英国政府，起义失败后，他在谷物集市被处以绞刑。

无视尸体上晃动的舌头

依然兴致勃勃。

钢笔画，淡水彩

把我们围拥在

高悬的客栈招牌下，

锋利的廊宇黑暗里。

现在是三点四十

尚有一丝光亮的

最后的下午。

嗅拉甘河的潮汐：

最后一次漫步

在可能性的强烈气息里。

北方的贮藏

而有些人在梦里确认
那如此折磨我们的鬼魂[①]

1. 根

叶的薄膜遮住了窗。
凭着街灯的光亮
你的身体迷恋
漂移的古坟，沉没的冰川岩。

而一切游移如梦，当你躲远
哀哭，离开每一座窗帘
紧闭的排屋，以及屋外种种
枪击、警笛和咕咕毒气的喧声

那里大地正在裂开。爱的触摸，

---

① 出自柯尔律治的《老水手谣》。

你在第一时间给予的暖热，

在我们古老的蛾摩拉①变得无助。

我们变成石头或被连根拔除。

黎明前我将为我们梦见

苍白的狙击手四处退散

而我走向灌木。

月光下我在潮水般的鲜血中浸入

一株曼德拉草，根深蒂固的人形戟，

大地的气囊，黑夜的肢体；

我伤害它潮湿刺鼻的土层

掩住耳朵不听它的尖叫声。

---

① 蛾摩拉（Gomorrah），《圣经·旧约·创世记》里的罪恶之城，
被上帝焚毁。

2. 无人地带

我弃甲曳兵，回避
他们伤口肆虐的雨篷，
他们手掌淌水的织网。

我一定要爬回去吗，
螺旋体，游荡在
挂满碎肉的铁丝和荆棘间，
去面对我染污的门阶
和死亡的肿块？
为什么我总是
姗姗来迟，去容忍
感染的缝线
和未接合的骨头？

3. 树 桩

我再度驶向磨难。
有时在烧毁的山墙内
壁炉染成烟灰色的涂层下
我看到贫困的人们在议事。
我该说些什么，若他们念叨起逝者？
我的伤口被烧灼，家园的黑树桩。

4. 没有避难所

万圣节前夜。萝卜人被砍下的头
透过破裂的瓶玻璃朝我们闪耀
冒烟并摇晃像毁船打劫者的灯笼。

丰收的死亡面具，万圣的嘲笑者
伴着烧焦的味道，黑夜里狗的红眼睛——
我们围坐并注视不神圣的光。

5. 火 种

我们捡燧石，
灰白，纹理布满尘土，

那么小，食指和拇指
捏着它们也会疼；

我们拨弄历史和家园的
冷念珠，洞口燃起

枝叶的火焰
在心灵的灯芯上震颤。

我们在石上击石，咔嗒，
只燃起微弱的火焰花粉

然后熄灭，指节撞击
同燧石一样频繁。

我们又知道些什么呢，
关于火种、烧焦的亚麻布和铁，

暮色下紧紧围坐一圈，
我们的拳头紧握，我们的希望萎缩？

什么能从我们死去的火成①岁月
击出一场大火？

现在我们蹲在冰冷的余烬上，
红着眼，火焰轻柔的雷声

和我们的思绪已尘埃落定。
我们直面苔原上呼啸的灌木

以新的历史，燧石和铁，
弃物，废料，指甲，犬齿。

---

① 火成（igneous），即火山爆发后，喷涌的熔岩冷却、变硬形
成岩石。

午 夜

自从有了职业战争——
尸体和腐肉
在雨中褪色——
狼在爱尔兰

灭绝。狼群
搜寻稀树草原和旷野
直到一个贵格派公子和他的狗
在基尔代尔的荒芜之地

杀死最后一只。
猎狼犬与低级
物种杂交,
森林被箍成酒桶。

雨今夜落在屋顶
打湿炭堤与石楠,
擦亮露出地表的
玄武岩和花岗岩,

滴入枯枝上的苔藓。
原来的兽穴浸了水。
爪垫不见了
或被晶莹微小的

寄生虫吞噬。
没有什么在喘息，吐舌，
挥汗。舌头
拴在我喉中。

图伦男子

一

总有一天我会去奥胡斯
去看他泥炭棕的头，
他眼睑的软豆荚，
他的尖皮帽。

在附近的平坦地带
他们把他挖出来，
他最后一顿冬粮粥
在他胃里结块，

赤身裸体，除了
帽子、绞索和腰带，
我将伫立良久。
女神的新郎，

她用她的金属项圈勒紧他
并打开她的沼泽，
那些黑暗的汁液
成就他圣徒的不坏之身，

割炭人的宝物
来自蜂房般的开采。
如今他弄脏的脸
安息在奥胡斯。

二

我可能冒着渎神的风险，
奉这片热锅似的沼泽
为我们的圣地并祈求
他使那些亡魂萌芽

被伏击的劳动者
血肉零落各处，
农舍院子里准备下葬的
穿袜子的尸体，

四位年轻兄弟
泄密的皮肤和牙齿
斑驳了枕木，沿着
铁轨绵延数里。

三

当他乘着死囚车
他悲哀的自由
多少也会传染我，开着车，
念地名

图伦，格劳巴勒，内伯尔加德，
看着村民指点
方向的手，
不懂他们的语言。

到达日德兰
在古老的杀人教区
我将感到迷失，
不快乐且如在自家。

内尔瑟斯①

美人，比如说立在泥炭里的桦树杈，
长长的纹理汇于凿开的裂隙；

沧桑、坦荡地接受风霜雪雨，
柳堤和小径指向石楠。

①日耳曼神话中的丰饶女神。

立石堆者

给柏瑞·库克[①]

他洗劫石头的巢，清空摇篮

让石子成为孤儿并让石

与石联姻：他不熟练的手

贪婪地挖空小山

和沼泽。固定，平衡，

就这样在布伦度过一整天，

他不是发现并添加石子

而是堆起一个又一个小石堆

并让一些石头带上他的印记。

他说起这些甚至怀着敬畏；

并与那里被触摸被安放的东西

产生奇异的联系，

意外的蜂房和迷你的城堡

---

① 柏瑞·库克（Barrie Cooke，1931–2014），爱尔兰画家，希尼
的朋友，曾为诗人画像。

插上三角旗，不属于任何人：
灯芯草和酢浆草、石楠的铃铛
在每一阵风过后飘扬。

筑路工

厚棉布手套硬得像树皮，
钻机把他的手腕固定在
页岩上：
那里路面起伏

拱起的部分倾斜
在慢车道，他站着
挥手让你停下。碎石路
蜿蜒而过的沼泽地

四年前吞没他的黄色
推土机，放倒它
连同湖上排屋和独木舟，
矛杆、斧头和骨针，

他不关心的一切。
天气或侮辱
不会让他松懈，
我的兄弟和守护人

埋头在碎石里

挖掘，沿着

布满伤痕与妊娠纹的

大地的弧线。

退伍老兵的梦

狄金森先生，我的邻居，

见过战争中最后的骑兵冲锋

并感染了最早的毒气

跛脚走入

他的头盔和卡其布军装。

他留意而不在意

毒气熏黄了他的纽扣

而在他的头附近

马队埋下它们的铁蹄。

他真正的恐惧是坏疽。

他和他的手在伤疤中醒来，

在他躺着的溃烂地上

一群蛆

施展它们的白魔法，

在他伤口的壕沟里

忙个不停。

征 兆

鱼面朝水流游动，
它的嘴张大，
整个脑袋打开像阀门。
你说"它病了"。

苍白结痂的疮
像一枚硬币
盘旋坠入水底，
扰落草上的淤泥。

我们如有神助
走在颤动的 T 台：
如今能保护我们的
也能慰藉阳光

刺伤的眼睛，
为湖泊解毒，
遣返
路上的老鼠。

第二部分

婚礼日

我很害怕。
那天连声音都停止了
而画面反反复复
旋转。为什么会有那些眼泪,

他①满脸狂烈的悲伤
在出租车外? 哀悼的
汁液在我们挥别的
客人心中涌起。

你在高高的蛋糕后歌唱
像一个被遗弃的新娘
坚持着,迷乱地,
行完婚礼仪式。

我走进男厕所
里面有一颗中箭的心
和一句爱的题词。就让我
睡在你的胸脯上去机场。

---

① 希尼的岳父。

新郎的母亲

她所记得的
是浴缸里
他发光的背，他的小靴子
在她脚边的一圈靴子里。

双手放在空空的膝间，
她听见一个女儿被迎进。
仿佛他被举起时双脚乱蹬
溜出她满是肥皂泡的怀抱。

从前肥皂能松开
结婚戒指
如今它永远地嵌入
她鼓掌的手里。

夏日之家

一

是垃圾堆的气味
还是酷热中什么

尾随我们，让夏天变了味，
一个臭烘烘的巢在某处孵育？

谁的错，我想知道，我审问
着魔的空气。

却恍然发现，
掀开门垫，

是幼虫，蠕动——
烫死，烫死，烫死。

二

我推开门，抱着
满怀的野樱桃和杜鹃花，

听见门廊传来她失落的
啜泣，时而尖厉时而嘶哑，
指责我的名，我的名。

哦，爱人，都怪我。

我们之间松散的花
聚拢，形成
某种五月的圣坛。
这些率真和衰落的花朵
很快会腐化为芳甜的圣油。

呵护。涂抹伤口。

三

哦，我们在舒适的被单下
遮盖好伤口

并仰面躺着仿佛冰冷的刀片
让我们喘不过气。

我越来越多地设想
亲密的疗愈，像此刻

你在淋浴间弯身
源源活水从你双乳的圣水钵倾泻。

四

随着最后
一次刺耳的驱动
长长的纹理开始
绽现并向前

裂开，再一次
我们摧毁
通往内心的
白色小径。

五

我的孩子们哭着熬过炎热的异国夜晚。
我们在地板上踱步，我的臭嘴拿你
出气，我们僵硬地躺着直到黎明
来到枕前，还有玉米，还有葡萄藤

向天光举起它饱满的负担。

昨日岩石歌唱，当我们在岩洞
古老而滴沥的黑暗中轻敲钟乳石——
此刻我们爱的召唤微渺如音叉。

小夜曲

爱尔兰的夜莺
是一种苇莺，
小小的鸟有着大嗓门
整夜聒噪不停。

不是你所期待的
一个音乐民族的声音。
我甚至还没听过一只——
就连猫头鹰，都没有。

我的小夜曲始终是
风里或梦里
乌鸦的破嗓音，
蝙蝠的喘息

或流浪的
长脚秧鸡的高射炮
迷失在无人地带的
联合收割机和化学品之间。

那么把奶瓶装满，亲爱的，

放进他们的婴儿床。

若他们真的吵醒我们，

好吧，苇莺也会。

梦游者

偷鸟蛋的手
和纱幔下的脸；

他哭着回来
泪水浸湿枕头

蛋黄的斑点布满
她的床单。

冬天的故事

一张苍白的脸在前灯
范围内摇曳并消失。
她从路边的围篱和铁丝网
逃走时划破的伤口还渗着
鲜血，黎明时他们
注视她赤身误入
牛群。灯笼、火把
和搜寻者轻松的闲聊
她起初躲闪：
此刻只有她的自己人
用毯子、绷带和白兰地
围拥她茫然的呜咽——
把他们头生的处女
接回家中的炉边和地板。
为什么跑掉啊，我们美丽的女儿，
袒胸逃离我们的家门？

不过，幸运的是，她回来了。
在一些夜晚，她跨过门槛
进入空荡荡的房子，温暖

她露湿的丰腴和褶皱，

睡在壁炉边的角落。

毕竟，他们是邻居。

作为邻居，当他们回来，

惊异但无恶意的

问候在他们

之间传递。她先来的，

所以看上去不是入侵者

而是，让所有来者成为宾客，

她仿佛从一场冬眠中

苏醒。微笑。胸前的手放了下来。

岸边女人

男人上山，女人上岸。

盖尔谚语

我穿过荒草呼啸的沙丘，那里
干燥松散的沙子正在风中筛沥，
我走在坚实的边缘。鸟蛤的
白麻壳、扇贝和牡蛎的白屋顶
贮藏月光，光线在海湾编织
又拆解。远处的礁石上
苍白的浮沫来了又去。

一条条鲭鱼拍死在甲板下
但每一次我们都把它们捞起，
僵冷的鱼尾随着第一口呼吸抽搐。
我的鱼线肯定探测到了暗流，
当我想拉钩，它重重地抵抗着
并朝着上方的光亮闪动、变肥。
他在船尾忙个不停。我大喊，
"这来得太容易，似乎不合理"，

但他解钩对付发狂的鱼

不说一字。然后突然平息，

我们已越过洄游地带，鱼线飞扬

像一阵失望，而我知道

我们已从海岬漂出了多远。

"数数你那边"，是他全部的言语

然后我看到鼠海豚厚厚的脊背

起伏翻滚仿佛海浪的飞轮，

光滑而闪亮。看到一座山

劈开水面也不会让我更惊愕，

不比眼前这迁徙的鱼群，

紧实黏稠的肌肉，从尾到口的环，

每一条都原形毕露，当它跃出

又潜入。

　　　　它们会攻击船。

我知道这种事并让他返港

但他不听，声称这是骗人

我的家人已被愚弄太久

他正要验证并平息这争论。

也许他会退缩，当油滑的拱背

朝我们推进：飘摇的敞篷船

溅起咸海水，我躺在下面尖叫，

感受木板传来的每一下重击和滑动，

对它们的水中狂嬉感到恶心。

我有时漫步这片海滨，为了感恩
或许也为了远离他在烤炉上
挥舞的烤鱼扦。海边才有
安全的味道，缓缓下倾的沙滩
窝藏的不过是竹蛏或螃蟹——
尽管我父亲记得沙丘上
出现过搁浅并喘息的鲸鱼尸体。
但今晚这些动人而结实的梦躺在
更暗更深处，远在海岬外。
迷失在一堆洗净的碎贝壳上，
在干燥的沙丘与垂涎的海浪之间，
我有权行走于这条休耕道，
月光与我影子之间的薄膜。

美人鱼

给肖恩·奥赫尔卡

一

她睡着了，冰冷的乳房
被潜流摇晃，
头发被扬起又放下。
缓缓荡漾的海藻
抛在小腿和大腿，
草编的脚环，漂流的
绳结抓住，又温柔地松开。

这是关于回家的
伟大初眠，壁炉
与床榻间的八载陆上岁月
被浸泡而凌乱。
她奇幻的衣裳
几乎还有海的颜色。

二

她梳头时他偷走了

她的衣裳：跟随

是她能做的一切。

他把衣裳藏在屋檐

并引诱她来到那里，四面墙，

暖地板，每晚男人的爱

海浪声近在咫尺。

她忍受哺乳和生育——

她别无选择——追忆

家的模样并排干

她嗓音中的潮音。

接着搭茅屋顶的人来了

随手把她的衣裳塞进干草间。

孩子们传来流言①。

三

晚风中，她走进

大海，裹在身上的

是他茅屋顶下的烟味，

稻草的潮气和薄薄的霉。

---

① "流言"（tales）与美人鱼的"尾巴"（tail）谐音，暗示美人鱼的秘密身份被揭穿。

她把他的秘密永远地
沉入海里，连同渔妇们

揭穿秘密的话音，
卧室里死死的控制，
对夜晚和明天的恐惧，
孩子们的刷子和梳子。
她睡着了，冰冷的乳房
被潜流摇晃。

灵　泊

巴利香农的渔夫们
昨晚捕捞了一个婴儿
连同一些鲑鱼。
一颗非法的卵，

被扔回水里的
一条小鱼。但我相信
当她站在沙滩
温柔地把他按在水里

直到她手腕冻僵的骨节
麻木如沙砾，
他依然是一条带钩的小鱼
把她撕裂。

她涉入水中
背负着她的十字。
他和鱼一同被捞起。
现在灵泊将是

灵魂闪耀的寒光

穿透遥远的咸水区。

即使基督未愈的手掌

也因刺痛而无法捕鱼。

私生子

他在鸡舍中被发现，
她把他关在那里。
他什么都不会说。

当灯火点亮，
一抹蛋黄色的光
投在他们的后窗，
茅舍里的孩子
把眼睛贴近缝隙——

鸡舍里的小男孩，
尖尖的脸像记忆中的
新月，你的照片依然
闪现像一只啮齿动物
在我心灵的地板，

小小的月牙人，
像狗被囚禁并忠守
院子的角落，
你孱弱的身形，光明，

轻盈，搅动尘埃，

蛛网，鸡舍下的
旧粪便
以及她晨晨昏昏
从活动门放进来的
残羹冷饭的气味。

在那些脚步声之后，沉寂；
守夜，孤独，斋戒，
未曾受洗的眼泪，
对光的不解之爱。
但如今你终于开口

以遥远的哑谜
讲述超越忍耐的事物，
你张口的无言证明着
爱无法企及的
月亮的距离。

晚　安

门闩抬起，一穴轮廓清晰的光
敞向院落。从低矮的门
他们俯身走进甜蜜的走廊，
然后径直穿过黑暗之墙。

水洼，卵石，门柱和门阶
稳稳置于一片明亮的区域。
直到她再次迈入，走出她的影子
并熄灭身后的一切。

初产母牛

我好久没有见过
胎盘挂在树篱上了
仿佛风刺痛
并涌起充血的眼泪。

母牛站在附近
她的头比她紧张倾斜的
脖子还沉重,
小牛狠狠吮吸乳房。

她浅浅的眼窝
倾溢出眼膜和液体。
她口鼻上温热的色斑
在湿鼻孔周围积聚赘物。

她的毛皮在风中保持温热。
她的大眼睛什么也不读。
她伤痛的旗语
在荆棘上裹紧并飘扬。

五　月

当我俯视桥下
鳟鱼正把天空掀翻
成碎片，墙上的
石头温暖我。

涉过绿茎，草耳
解开并受伤
（小小的汁液自喷井）
我的鞋尖闪烁在

爱尔兰柔软的
囟门。我应该穿
皮鞋，皮毛紧贴皮肤，
走过这片土地：

那儿不是有矿泉吗，
墙顶上草木葱茏、垂悬？
然后泉水涌出
流过碎石堤。

我外出寻找那村庄，

它低矮的窗台散发

酢浆草和毛茛的芳香，

夏夜里沼泽地发光。

炉 边

永远有故事讲述那些
盘旋于灌木<u>丛</u>或草原尽头的
光亮；也许是冷犄角的山羊
羽毛般腾入月亮；锁链

在午夜的路上叮当。然后也许
聊天就会围绕那门水上
技艺，灯下捕鱼，我也会
像月亮那样用手电筒照射溪水

被舔舐的黑毛皮，我的左臂张开
去接纳阻碍渔网的沉重
涌流。那究竟是灯光
在旋涡上扭曲还是异象

灵光一闪？稳住光线，
清醒过来，它们在道晚安。

黎　明

有人拉开窗帘。
窗边的灌木
闪光，清新的绿叶
摇摇晃晃。

我们停在路中央
等红绿灯，鸽群在
街上，如四散的
卵石，咕咕落地。

我们时速五英里。
叽叽喳喳的会谈
正在进行，学者们
辩论，通宵达旦

一种庞贝式的寂静。
当我们悄悄去海边，
橱窗里的模特注视我们。
我独自抽身，来到

滨螺和鸟蛤的碎屑上

发现自己突然

寸步难移，否则会踩碎

众多不堪一击的塔楼。

旅　行

牛群撑着它们的头
走进午后烈日，
甜瓜像黄铜布满山坡：

谁读得远谁就读得
远超我们，我们沉睡的孩子
以及落在焦草上的微尘。

西　行

于加利福尼亚

我坐在兰德·麦克纳利出版的
《月球官方地图》下——
蛙皮的颜色，
放大的毛孔

张开，其中一个叫作
"皮蒂斯楚斯"，与目光齐平——
让人想起在多尼戈尔的
最后一晚，我的影子

在她瘦削的清辉下
洁净地投在白石灰墙，
院子里的鹅卵石
亮白如卵。

夏季是一次自由落体
终结在那里，
西部的圆形剧场
空荡。受难日那天

我们启程
经过午后商店拉起的遮阳篷
静静的教堂外静止的汽车，
斜倚在墙边的单车；

我们驶过，
一种逐渐减弱的扰动
如铃锤击响在
空空的祭坛

会众俯身朝向
钉着钉子的十字。
什么钉子落在那个时辰？
道路如线轴松解，松解，

衰落的光如钓线
抛在
粼粼的水面。
月球的圣痕①下

六千英里以外，
我想象不受扰乱的尘埃，
逐渐松弛的引力，
基督用他的双手负重。

———————————
① 圣痕，状如耶稣被钉死在十字架后留在身上的伤痕。

北　方

1975

目录

致　谢

作者由衷感谢美国爱尔兰基金会在一九七三至一九七四年间授予本人年度文学奖，并给予资助。

感谢以下报刊的编辑，本书中的一些诗歌曾首发于这些报刊：

《安泰》、《爱尔兰艺术》、《堤道》(BBC 三台)、《文汇》、《流放》、《海伯尼亚》、《爱尔兰新闻》、《爱尔兰时报》、《爱尔兰大学评论》、《詹姆斯·乔伊斯季刊》、《倾听者》、《新评论》、《凤凰》、《泰晤士报文学增刊》；

感谢以下诗选的编者：

《费伯爱尔兰诗选》、《新诗：1972–1973》和《新诗：1973–1974》(哈钦森)，《探测：1972 年度诗选》(布莱克斯塔夫，贝尔法斯特)。

八首诗曾发表在限量版诗集《沼泽诗》(彩虹出版社)。

莫斯浜：献给玛丽·希尼①的两首诗

1. 阳 光

有一种阳光照亮的缺席。

戴头盔的水泵在院子里

热它的铁，

水在吊桶里

呈现蜜色

而太阳

像一个平烤盘

靠在墙边冷却

在每一个漫长的下午。

就这样，她的手

在面板上忙碌，

变红的烤炉

向她散发铁板的

---
① 希尼的姑姑。

热量，她站在窗前
身上的围裙
沾满面粉。

她时而用鹅毛掸
拂拭面板，
时而坐下，双膝摊开，
指甲泛白

小腿布满斑疹：
这里有空闲
再一次，司康随着
两个钟头的嘀嗒膨胀。

这里还有爱
像锡匠的小铲
把它的微光
沉入面缸。

2. 种子切割者

他们仿佛远在千百年前。勃鲁盖尔，
你会认出他们，如果我写得真。
他们跪在树篱下围成半圈儿
防风墙后，风正突破防禁。
他们是种子切割者。叶芽的褶边
已从埋在稻草下的土豆种里
窥探。他们有的是时间消磨，
于是慢慢消磨时间。每柄利刃
懒洋洋地对切每块根茎，它们
落在掌中：一道乳白的微光，
以及，中央，一抹幽暗的水印。
哦，时令的习俗！在他们头上
在金黄的金雀花下，构思画作，
把我们都画在那里，我们这些无名者。

第一部分

安　泰

当我卧于大地
我起身如清晨的玫瑰满面红光。
比赛中我设法倒在拳击场
　　用沙子摩擦自己

　　那样做很有效
犹如灵丹妙药。我不能断奶，
离开大地蜿蜒的轮廓，她的水脉。
　　在我下方的穴巢，

　　周围是根与岩，
我在黑夜子宫的摇篮里
每一条动脉都得到哺育
　　宛若一座小山。

　　让每个新英雄前来
寻找金苹果和阿特拉斯。
他必须与我角力再由此
　　进入荣誉的国度

比肩天生的王者：

他可以撂倒我让我重获生息

但他不要指望，把我举离大地，

　　我的升起，我的坠落。

（1966）

贝尔德格

"它们不断涌现
被视为外来物"——
独眼而无害，
躺在他屋外，
来自沼泽的石磨。

揭开泥炭的眼帘
发现这瞳孔正梦见
新石器时代的麦粒！
当他剥光覆盖的沼泽
柔软堆叠的众多世纪

散开如发帘：
那里有最初的耕迹，
石器时代的田野，坟墓
有托梁、草皮和墓室，
地上铺着干草。

风景变成化石，
它的石砌图案

重现于我们眼前
梅奥的石墙。
我转身离开前

他谈起延续，
生命的合一，
他的家，清空了石头，
如何以铁、燧石和青铜：
积聚一圈圈年轮。

于是我谈起莫斯浜，
沼泽名。"但苔藓？"
他以更古老的斯堪的纳维亚旋律
穿越我故乡的音乐。
我说起它的根基如何

变化无常如音响
而我那分叉的根
又如何源自那片土壤，
使"浜"成为英伦的"堡"，
殖民者围起的山岗，

抑或发现庇护所
并认为它很爱尔兰，

固执甚至过时。

"但你树上的斯堪的纳维亚年轮？"

我把一座古老磨坊的谷物，

放入石磨的眼，

而我心灵的眼睛看到

世界之树起于平衡之石，

石磨堆叠如椎骨，

骨髓碾压成沉滓。

葬礼仪式

一

我肩负某种成年的责任，
走进屋去抬逝世
亲属的棺材。
他们一直被放在

染污的房间，
他们的眼睑晶莹，
双手白如面团
铐在玫瑰念珠里。

他们浮肿的指节
没了皱纹，指甲
黯淡，手腕
顺从地倾斜。

红藻棕的裹尸布，
絮棉的绸缎褥：
我谦恭地跪下，
敬重这一切，

当蜡融化淌下
形成烛的血脉，
火焰彷徨于
我身后彷徨的

女人们。
而永远，在某个角落，
有棺材盖，
钉头装饰着

小小的发光十字。
亲爱的滑石面具，
必须把他们的冰屋额头
亲个够

然后钉子钉下，
每一场葬礼的
黑冰川
艰难离去。

二

如今每当新闻传来

邻里相杀的消息
我们渴望仪式，
约定俗成的节奏：

葬礼队伍克制的
脚步，蜿蜒走过
每一个窗帘紧闭的家庭。
我想复原

博因的巨大墓室，
在残留杯印的石头下
准备一座坟冢。
从小街和支路

汩汩涌出的私家汽车
小心翼翼驶进队伍，
整个村子都调频于
千万台引擎

压低的鼓声。
梦游的女人们，
留在家中，游移于
空荡荡的厨房

想象我们迟缓驶向

坟冢的胜利。

安静如巨蟒

在草木丛生的林荫道逶迤，

队伍把它的尾巴拖出

北方的山隘

而它的头已伸进

史前巨石的入口。

三

当他们把石头放

回它的入口

我们将再度北上

经过斯特兰和卡灵湾，

记忆的反刍

一度减轻，世仇的

仲裁平息，

想象那些山底的人

被处死如贡纳①

优美地躺在

他的陵墓中，

尽管死于暴力

且没有复仇。

人们说他在唱诵

荣耀之诗

四盏灯燃烧

在墓室的角落：

陵墓开启，当他转身

以欢颜

望向明月。

---

① 贡纳（Gunnar），十世纪冰岛的一位族长，战无不胜的英雄，出现在《尼雅尔萨迦》的前半部分。《尼雅尔萨迦》讲述世仇与复仇的后果。

北　方

我回到一处长滩，

海湾被锤打的蹄铁，

却只发现大西洋

雷霆万钧的世俗威力。

我面对着冰岛

毫无魔力的邀约，

格陵兰可悲的

殖民地，而突然间

那些传说中的入侵者，

那些躺在奥克尼和都柏林的人

与他们生锈的长剑

比试高低，

那些在石船墓

坚固船底的人，

那些被砍死并在冰释的

溪流沙砾中闪闪发光的人

是大海振聋发聩的

警示之音，再一次

在暴力和显灵中升起。

维京长舟的游舌

浮泛着后视的目光——

它诉说着托尔[①]的大锤

挥向地理和贸易，

愚蠢的交合与复仇，

阿尔庭[②]的仇恨与

背后议论，谎言与女人，

疲惫名曰和平，

记忆酝酿流血。

它说："躺在

文字秘藏里，钻探

你盘绕而闪耀的

头脑的犁沟。

———————

[①] 托尔（Thor），北欧神话中的雷神，其所向无敌的武器是大锤，既可以摧毁一座山，又能带来祝福、繁育和复活。他以大锤保护世界，无论击中什么，大锤都会返回手中。维京时代，锤形饰物为战士所爱。

[②] 阿尔庭（Althing），古老的冰岛议会，建立于九三〇年，乃世界上最早的议会。

在黑暗中创作。
于漫长的进击中
期待北极光
而非光的瀑流。

保持目光澄澈
如冰柱的气泡，
信任你双手所知的
粗砺宝藏的触感。"

维京人的都柏林：样品

一

它可能是一块颌骨
或肋骨或从更结实的
部位割下的一部分：
总之，它上面刻着

小小的线条，用于
施魔法的笼或架。
像孩子的舌头
追随他举步

维艰的书写，
像一条鳗鱼
被吞入一篮鳗鱼，
线条对自己着迷，

避开那只
喂它的手，
飞翔的喙，
游泳的鼻孔。

二

这些是样品，
手艺的奥秘
在骨上即兴发挥：
树叶，动物寓言，

错综复杂的线条
如祖先和贸易的
网络路线。
这一切必须

放大展示
才看出鼻孔
是迁徙的船头
吸嗅利菲河，

似天鹅颈伸向浅滩，
将自己掩藏于
鹿角梳，骨胸针，
钱币，砝码，秤盘。

三

像一柄长剑
插入它葬身的
湿粘土，
龙骨牢牢插入

堤岸的斜坡，
它叠搭的船体
有脊梁和爆破音
就像都柏林。

而现在我们伸手
去触摸椎骨的残片，
栏架的肋骨，
母乳的秘窖——

去触摸这件
孩子雕刻的样品，
一艘长舟，浮动的
迁徙线。

四

它进入我的手写体，
变成连笔字，揭开
一道兽形的航迹，
一条思想的蠕虫

我跟随它进入淤泥。
我是丹麦人哈姆雷特，
持头骨者，讲寓言者，
国家腐败的

嗅探者，染上
它的毒性，
纠缠于魂灵
与深情，

谋杀与虔诚，
跳进坟墓
以恢复清醒，
犹豫不决，喋喋不休。

五

来和我飞吧，
来嗅探风，
以维京人的
看家本领——

邻里的、记分的
杀手，预言者
和讲价者，投机者，
恨与利的囤积者。

他们以屠夫的沉着
铺开你的双肺
为你的双肩制作
温暖的羽翼。

古老的父辈，请与我们同在。
古老而精明的估算师，
评估世仇并选定场址
埋下伏击或建立城池。

六

"你可曾听说过,"
吉米·法雷尔[1]说,
"都柏林那座城市里
有各种各样的头骨?

白头骨和黑头骨
还有黄头骨,一些
牙齿齐全,另一些
却只有一颗,"

而合成的历史
就在"一个或许在洪水中
淹死的老丹麦人"的
头盖骨上。

我的文字舔舐
鹅卵石码头,去猎寻,
像爱尔兰古老的鞋履,
轻踏头骨覆盖的土地。

---

[1] 约翰·辛格戏剧《西方世界的花花公子》中的人物。

挖掘的骷髅

仿波德莱尔

一

码头一带尘土飞扬

你发现被埋没的解剖图例

那些书本泛黄如木乃伊

沉睡在被遗忘的板条箱，

图画有一种奇崛的美

仿佛那制图者曾经

以庄严肃穆的心境

将解剖的哀思描绘——

对骨骼周围的红泥地

展开神秘而坦诚的研究。

比如这个：被剥皮的人与骷髅

挖掘大地如同苦役。

二

一伙悲哀的鬼魂，

你们去皮的肌肉如编织的莎草
你们的脊梁弓向土中的铁锹
锋刃，我耐心的人们，

告诉我，当你们辛苦劳动
为击破这无情的土壤，
你们可要填满什么谷仓？
那从墓地拽你们的是什么监工？

或者你们是真理的标记，
死亡的解除者，被拖出狭小的囚室
并剥去裹尸布睡衣，为了告知：
"这就是对永恒安息

信念的酬报。甚至死亡
也说谎。虚空骗人。
我们并非像秋叶那样凋零
并安详睡去。背叛的呼吸让

尘身复苏，放我们出去，
通过被剥皮的额头的汗水
我们谋死；当流血的脚背
找到铁锹才是我们唯一的安息。"

骨头梦

一

白骨被发现
于草场：
粗砺、多孔的
触觉语言

及其草丛中
泛黄的肋纹印迹——
小小的船葬。
死如顽石，

被发现的燧石，
金锭般的白垩，
我再次触摸它，
我把它绕于

心灵的弹弓
掷向英格兰
并追随它坠落
在陌生的田野。

二

骨宅：
一具骨架
在语言的
古老地牢。

我通过
语辞回溯，
伊丽莎白时代的华盖。
诺曼人的徽章，

普罗旺斯多情的
五月花
教士们爬满常青藤的
拉丁文

抵达吟游诗人的
铿锵，辅音如
铁的爆破
劈开诗行。

三

在语法
和变格的
富饶金库中
我找到骨宅，

它的炉火，长凳，
篱笆和房椽，
在那里灵魂
也要在屋顶空间

盘旋一会儿。
一个小瓦罐
给头脑，
一口热锅

为繁殖，
在中央摇晃：
爱巢，血穴，
梦的树荫。

四

回来吧
经由语文学和隐喻词，
重新进入记忆
那里骨窝

是草地上的
一个爱巢。
我捧着恋人的头
像一枚水晶

并通过凝视
骨化自己：我是她
陡坡上的碎石，
刻在她丘陵的

白垩巨人。
很快我的手，在她脊椎
下沉的沟渠上
移向关口。

五

而我们终于
彼此相拥
在防御工事的
双唇之间。

当我出于
好玩去估量
她指节的铺路石，
她双肘的

人字梯，
她前额的壁垒
还有锁骨的
窄门，

我已开始步测
她肩上的哈德良
长城，梦想
梅登堡。

六

一天早晨在德文郡
我发现一只死鼹鼠
身上还缀着露珠。
我原以为鼹鼠

是大骨架的犁刀
但眼前这只，
又小又冷
像凿刀的手柄。

有人告诉我，"吹吧，
把它头上的皮毛吹到后面。
那些小点点
是眼睛。

去感受那肩膀。"
我触摸小小的遥远的奔宁山脉，
青草的毛皮与纹理
向南奔去。

到绿荫中来

我摸索的双手
触到野蔷薇和纠缠的野豌豆，
掠过那些被钱币秘藏
撑破的砂囊

前往黑树荫皇后之所在，
她正等待
我的破解。逃离泥炭贪吃
的黑嘴，锋利的柳枝

温柔退散。
我剥开外皮看见
头骨的钵，
每一朵卷发的潮湿皱褶

红得像狐狸尾巴，
她喉咙上还有护喉甲
留下的痕迹。而清泉
开始在她周围泛滥。

我掠过

河床淘濯的

黄金梦

前往她维纳斯骨的金锭。

沼泽女王

我躺着等待
在泥炭表层与庄园围墙之间，
在石楠丛生的平原
与玻璃尖齿的岩石之间。

我的身体是盲文
那些隐秘的力量触摸我：
黎明的阳光抚摸我头顶
又在我脚下变冷，

透过我的织体和皮肤
冬的涓流
消化我，
无知的根须

沉思并死于
对胃和臼窝的
洞穴探测。
我躺着等待

在多砂的沼泽底，

我的大脑渐黯，

一罐卵

在地下发酵

梦想波罗的海琥珀。

我指甲下是淤紫的浆果，

生命力的贮藏

在骨盆的陶皿内减少。

我的王冠长了龋齿，

宝石落入

泥炭的浮冰

像历史的轴承。

我的绶带是起皱的

黑冰川，染色的织品

和腓尼基人的刺绣

在我乳房的柔软

冰碛上腐烂。

我知道冬的冷

像峡湾用鼻子

蹭我的大腿——

浸湿的羽翼，沉重的
兽皮绷带。
我的头颅冬眠
在我头发的湿巢。

他们抢走我头发。
割泥炭者的铁锹
把我修剪
并剥光

重新给我蒙上面纱
并在我头边和脚边的
石框之间轻柔地
填充松软的天然材料。

直到一位贵族夫人贿赂他。
我的发辫，
一条黏糊糊的
沼泽脐带，被剪断

于是我从黑暗中起身，
砍破的骨，头颅器皿，
磨损的针脚，发缕，
泥滩上的点点微光。

格劳巴勒男子[①]

他仿佛被浇注了
柏油，躺在
泥炭的枕上
似乎在哭泣

他自己这黑河流。
他双腕的纹理
如同沼泽橡，
圆圆的脚踵

像玄武岩的卵。
他的脚背已萎缩
冰冷如天鹅脚
或潮湿如沼泽根。

他的屁股是河蚌的
分水岭和贝壳包，
他的脊柱如鳗鱼

----

① 一九五二年四月，在丹麦格劳巴勒地区的沼泽里发现的男子
尸体。

困于闪光的淤泥。

头昂起，
下巴是面甲
高举过他被割喉的
通风口

那里已晒黑、僵硬。
风干的伤口
向内张开，通往幽暗的
接骨木浆果色地带。

面对他鲜活的表情
谁会说"尸体"？
面对他不透光的安睡
谁会说"死人"？

还有他生锈的头发，
乱糟糟的一团
仿佛胎儿的毛发。
我最初看到他扭曲的脸

是在一张照片中，
探出泥炭的

头颅和肩膀，

淤紫如被产钳夹出的婴儿，

但如今他完好地

躺在我的记忆里，

甚至他指甲的

红色角质，

也悬于天平，

连同美与暴力：

连同那精准地待在

盾牌范围内

垂死的高卢人，

连同每个被割喉被抛弃

被蒙面的牺牲品的

实际重量。

惩　　罚

我能感到
她脖子后面拉紧的
绳索，吹在她
赤裸前胸的风。

风将她的乳头
吹成琥珀珠，
风摇撼她肋骨
脆弱的索具。

我能看见她沉溺
在沼泽中的尸体，
加重下沉的石头，
漂浮的柳条和树枝。

枝条下，她首先
是被剥皮的小树
被挖出来
橡树骨，脑木桶：

她剃光的头

像收割后的黑麦田，

她的蒙眼布是弄脏的绷带，

她的绞索是指环

为贮藏

爱的回忆。

小奸妇，

在他们惩罚你之前

你有着亚麻色的头发，

营养不良，你的

柏油黑的脸很美。

我可怜的替罪羊，

我几乎爱上你

但也会投下，我知道，

缄默的石子。

我是技艺高超的偷窥者

窥探你头颅暴露的

幽暗的蜂房，

你肌肉的韧带组织

和你所有被编号的骨头：

我也曾哑然伫立

当你那些叛逆的姐妹，

头上被浇柏油，

在围栏边啜泣，

我也会默许

文明的义愤

但深知这是严苛、

部族的私密复仇。

奇异的果实

女孩的头颅像被掏空的葫芦。

鸭蛋脸，肤如梅干，牙如梅核。

他们梳理她头发的湿蕨

并向人们展示它的盘绕，

让空气吹拂她坚韧的美。

油脂的脑袋，脆弱的宝藏：

她破损的鼻子黑似泥炭块，

她的眼窝空洞如旧采石场的水坑。

西西里的狄奥多罗斯承认

他对此类事物已渐渐适应：

被杀，被忘，无名，可怕的

被斩首的女孩，逼视大斧

与教皇宣福，逼视

人们开始隐隐流露的崇敬。

亲　缘

一

晾晒场上象形文字的
泥炭让我与那个
被绞死的受害者以及
那蕨中爱巢产生亲缘，

我步行穿过源头
像一条狗
在厨房草垫上翻转
它荒野的记忆：

沼泽地震动，
当我走过
灯芯草和石楠
水滋滋发出咬舌音。

我爱这泥炭表层，
它漆黑的切口，
过程和仪式
被幽禁的秘密；

我爱在这

地面上弹跳，

每个斜坡如绞刑架的落板，

每个敞开的深潭

是陶瓷

未缄之口，饮月者，

无法被肉眼

所探测。

二

泥潭，湿地，泥泞：

黏液的列国，

冷血动物，泥爪垫

和脏卵的领地。

但沼泽

意为柔和，

无风的雨坠落，

琥珀的瞳仁。

反刍的土地，

消化软体动物
和种荚，
深沉的花粉仓。

地窖，圣骨墓，
阳光库，防腐剂
保存还愿供品
和被砍死的亡徒。

不知满足的新娘。
吞刀饮剑者，
珠宝匣，垃圾堆，
历史的浮冰。

将剥去黑暗面的
土地，
筑巢地，
我心灵的内陆。

三

我发现一个炭锹
隐蔽在蕨草下，
平躺着，上面长满

绿雾般的再生草。

当我抬起它
植被柔软的嘴唇
嘟囔并分开，
一条黄褐色凹痕

在我脚下显露
如一层蜕掉的皮，
当我把它立在土中
它的柄潮湿

并开始在
阳光下蒸腾。
而现在他们使这座
方尖碑结对：

在乱石中，
在芒毛丛生的石堆下
一个爱巢被搅动，
柔夷花序和沼泽棉颤抖

当他们抬起
分叉的橡树枝：

我站在数百年来的边缘
面对一位女神。

四

这中心稳固
并蔓延，
淤水坑与育苗床，
一汪羊水

和一座融化的坟。
秋天的母亲们
变酸变深沉，
壳与叶的发酵

加深它们的赭石色。
苔藓到了生死关头，
石楠撒籽，
蕨类沉积

其古铜色。
这是大地的元音
梦想着它
花中雪中的根，

变化的天气
与季节，
被风吹落的果实织构
它腐化的地面。

我从这一切中生长出来
像一株垂柳
俯向
引力的食欲。

五

泥炭车轮
手工雕刻的轮缘
埋在一堆
炭霉中，

后挡板的
丘比特之弓，
护栏车厢
嵌入的唇：

我神化那位

驾车人，

运货马车之神，

壁炉的喂养者。

我有幸成为他的

跟班，背着

面包和饮料，

他路上的扈从。

当夏日已尽

主妇们遗弃农田

我们外出游荡，

人们致敬、让路。

看我们沿着

山楂点亮的树篱前进，

当他对我说话

我感到男子汉的骄傲。

六

而你，塔西陀，

看我怎样在可怖的死人

成堆的沼泽古堡

种植我的小树林：

一片荒芜的和平。
我们的大地母亲
因染上她的信众之血
而酸辛，

他们躺在她神圣的
心中汩汩淌血
而军团从防御墙上
四处盯视。

回到这座
"海洋之岛"吧，
这里什么都不够。
读伤亡者和遇难者

被埋葬的面容吧；
公平地报道我们，
我们怎样为了
共同利益而屠戮

并剃光那些
恶名者的头，
女神怎样吞噬
我们的爱与怖。

海洋对爱尔兰的爱

一

操着浓重的德文郡口音，

雷利^①把侍女推到一棵树边

如爱尔兰被推向英格兰

并向内陆猛冲

直至她所有的海滨都喘不过气：

"沃沃尔特爵爵士！沃沃尔特爵爵士！"

他是水，他是洋，掀起

她的裙撑如一幔海草掀起

在风口浪尖。

二

然而他华丽的羽冠倾向辛西娅

---

① 沃尔特·雷利爵士（Sir Walter Raleigh，1552–1618），英国
军事家、政治家、冒险家，同时也是文艺复兴时期著名诗人。
在英国对北美殖民、镇压爱尔兰叛乱和击败西班牙无敌舰队方
面发挥了重要作用。雷利在诗中的"辛西娅"（见组诗第二首）
暗指伊丽莎白一世女王。

即使它的波峰涌向

丽河与布莱克沃特河。

那是些积水地带，他将把

斗篷铺在她面前。在伦敦，他的名字

将在水上升起，也升起在这些幽暗的渗流：

斯摩维克被播种下六百具教皇党人

开口的尸体，"前所未见的英勇

善良的大人物。"

三

被蹂躏的侍女用爱尔兰语抱怨，

海洋驱散了她的舰队梦，

西班牙王子洒了金子

并负了她。英语的抑扬格

鼓点击打树林，她的诗人们

沦陷如奥南。灯芯草的光，蘑菇肉，

她从它们沉睡的环抱中消逝

成为卷发的气息和露珠，

被占有和反复被占有的土地。

幻　象

他向她求爱

以一种颓废的甜蜜手段

像风的元音

吹过榛树林：

"你是黛安娜吗……？"

而他是不是亚克托安，

他的挽歌

是雄鹿发情时声嘶力竭的呼喊？

联合法案

今夜，最初的胎动，脉搏，
仿佛沼泽地的雨势增强，
滑落并泛滥：沼泽的爆破，
一道深深的伤口裂开蕨床。
你的背是东岸坚定的轮廓
而双臂与双腿伸向
你平缓的群山外。我抚摸
这隆起的省份，我们的往昔在此生长。
我是你身后的高大王国
你既不引诱也不轻看。
征服是个谎言。年长的我
承认你半独立的海岸
在其边界内我的遗产
正不可阻挡地达至峰巅。

而如今我依然是帝国
男人，留下你承受疼痛，

殖民地正在渐渐撕破，

攻城槌，从内部爆发轰鸣。

此举刺激了固执的第五纵队

其立场正变得一意孤行。

你心底的他的心是战鼓

集结力量。他那双寄生

并且无知的小小拳头已然

在你的边界敲击而我知道它们

在水对岸向我扣动扳机。没有条款

能让我预见完全治愈你布满伤痕

和妊娠纹的身体，治愈那再度

让你破裂的，像开垦地，痛楚。

凯弗山的订婚

炮火把它的疑问吠出凯弗山
玄武岩的侧影保持它的凝视
向南：骄傲，新教且北方，男性。
亚当未被触及，未受性别冲击。

他们依然在此鸣枪祝福新郎。
那天早上我驱车外出为躺在
我爱人的幽居、她的豆荚和金雀花，
他们在我的汽车上方开火庆祝。

赫拉克勒斯与安泰

天生的王者，

斩蛇者，除粪者，

他一心想着金苹果，

他的未来挂满战利品，

赫拉克勒斯有办法

应对抵抗和以土地

为食的黑色力量。

安泰，拥抱土地者，

终于断奶：

跌倒即重生

但此刻他被举起——

挑战者的智慧

是光的马刺，

一柄蓝叉戟把他挑起

离开他必要的环境

陷入失落与本源

之梦——摇篮里的黑暗，

河流的脉络，他力量的

秘密沟壑，

洞穴与地下通道的

孵化地，

他把这一切遗赠给

挽歌诗人。巴洛尔将死去，

还有比尔特诺斯和坐牛。①

赫拉克勒斯举起双臂

形成无情的 V，

他的胜利未被

他所撼动之力攻击，

他把安泰斜斜举起

高如轮廓鲜明的山脊，

一个熟睡的巨人，

流离失所者的流食。

---

① 巴洛尔（Balor）、比尔特诺斯（Byrhtnoth）和坐牛（Sitting Bull）是三位反抗外来入侵而死的英雄人物。巴洛尔是爱尔兰神话中的独眼巨人。比尔特诺斯（931–991）是埃塞克斯的贵族，在马尔登之战中领导盎格鲁–撒克逊人民反抗维京人的侵略而遭杀害。坐牛（1831–1890）是北美印第安人首领，在反抗白人入侵的战斗中被杀。

第二部分

未被公认的立法者的梦

阿基米德认为，如果找到正确的位置安放他的杠杆，他就可以撬动地球。比利·亨特说，当人猿泰山从树上跳落，他也撼动了世界。

我把撬棍插进政体与法令石基下我所知的一条裂隙，我凭借一根秘密爬藤纵身跃入巴士底狱。我那被冤屈的人民从囚笼中发出欢呼。看门狗被解除口套，一个士兵把枪口对准我耳际，我被迫站立，双眼被蒙蔽，双手举过头顶，我仿佛在一个吊坠刑具上荡来荡去。

指挥官挥手示意我坐下。"我很荣幸将一位诗人加入我们的名单。"他既好笑又真诚。"不管怎样，你在这儿更安全。"

囚室中，我伸开双臂把自己挤进角落并施压，我跳上水泥石板测探。刚才出现在门洞里的可是你的眼睛？

无论你说什么什么也别说

一

我写下这首诗，在遇见一位
英国记者后，他正四处搜寻
"对爱尔兰事件的看法"。我回归
冬日营地，这里坏新闻不再是新闻，

这里媒体党和键盘侠指点嗅猎，
这里变焦镜头、录音机和盘绕的电线
凌乱堆放在酒店。时代脱了节
但我倾向于信任玫瑰珠串

一如我倾向政客和记者之流
匆匆写就的各种便笺和分析
他们草草书写这场漫长的战斗
从瓦斯和抗议到炸药和扳机，

他们根据自己的脉搏证明"升温"、
"反冲"和"镇压"，"临时党"，
"两极化"和"旷日持久的仇恨"。
但我生活在这里，我也生活在这里，我大嚷，

熟练地用礼貌的话语同礼貌的邻人
在高空钢丝上谈论最初的无线电讯，
吮吸那些公认、陈腐而精心的驳论
所蕴含的虚假意味、铁石气氛：

"哦，当然，这真丢人，我同意。"
"到哪儿才是尽头？""事态越来越恶劣。"
"他们是杀人犯。""拘留，合情合理……"
"理智的声音"正变得声嘶力竭。

二

人们死在眼前。在炸毁的街头和家园
葛里炸药是司空见惯的音效：
像那人说的，当凯尔特人获胜，"今晚
罗马教皇是幸福的人。"他的信众怀抱

内心最深处的猜想，以为异教徒
终于唯命是从并来到火刑柱前。
我们在靠近火焰的地方颤抖但并不
打算真正点火。我们永远

唯利是图。长期捡食残羹冷炙，

冷如女巫的乳头，硬得难以下咽，

依然使我们对边界问题言辞不实：

开明的教皇党人的声音听来空泛

当它被扩大并混杂于那朝朝暮暮

撼动所有心脏和窗户的轰鸣。

（此处很想押韵于"分娩的痛楚"

并在我们的苦难中诊断一场重生

但那就意味着忽视其他症状。

昨晚你并不需要一台听诊器

去倾听奥兰治鼓对皮尔斯和教皇

同样过敏而发出的反胃呃逆。）

在各个方位"小小的排连"结集——

这个词组是克鲁斯·奥布莱恩①转引

伟大的反击者伯克之语——而我坐在这里

焦灼地渴望既是鱼钩也是诱饵的诗文

来诱使部族的鱼群成为箴言

和秩序。我相信我们任何人

---

① 克鲁斯·奥布莱恩（Conor Cruise O'Brien，1917–2008），爱尔兰政治家、作家与学者，认同埃德蒙·伯克的思想传统。

都能同偏执与虚伪划清界线，

只要路线正确，坚似铜金。

三

当然，"这里从不提及宗教"。

"你通过眼神辨识他们"，并守口如瓶。

"一方同另一方一样糟"，没有更糟。

基督，是时候让某个小小的漏洞

涌现于荷兰人建造的大堤

以便阻拦那追随谢默斯的危险浪潮。

然而尽管拥有这技能和伏案的手艺

我却无能为力。家喻户晓

如北方的缄默，封口布紧锁地点

与时代：是的，是的。"六小郡"是我的歌

在那里要保全自己你只须保全颜面

且无论你说什么什么也别说。

和我们相比，烟雾信号高谈阔论：

用欺诈的手段分辨姓名和教派，

根据地址进行微妙的区分

这个规则几乎无一例外

诺曼、肯和西德尼代表新教之流，

而谢默斯（叫我肖恩）必信教皇。

哦，密码之乡，握手、眨眼和点头，

思想开放之地，开放如一张罗网，

那里舌头蜷缩，如火焰下的灯芯，

那里我们多半，藏身于木马，

被囚禁被限制如狡猾的希腊人，

被围困于围困，低语莫尔斯电码。

四

今天早晨从露湿的高速公路

我看到关押拘留犯的新营地：

一枚炸弹在路边留下一处

新土坑，而那边的树丛里

机枪哨界定真实的防御。

那里有你在低地常见的白雾

而这似曾相识，如讲述十七号

战俘营的电影，一场无声的噩梦。

死之前可有生？这句话被粉笔

写在市中心的墙上。胜任苦痛，

患难与共，一箪食，一瓢饮，

我们再度拥抱卑微的宿命。

自由民

的确，在罗马帝国早期，奴隶制最接近合理：
因为一个来自落后种族的人可以由此进入文明
的领地，接受教育和行业培训，成为社会的有
用之才。

R. H. 巴罗，《罗马人》

年复一年在拱门下臣服，
自由来自一纸文凭和学位证书，
我的骨螺是大斋节的紫色
日历上所有的斋戒和禁欲。

"记住，人，你来自微尘。"
我将跪下接受灰烬的烙印，
丝绸的摩擦，尘埃的点染——
我也受制于人如我所有的族员。

一个带有尘记的居民，挥之不去，
在精致的优越者身上我找不到这印记：
他们那种打量、审视的眼色
像八目鳗牢牢盯住我发霉的前额。

然后诗歌抵达那座城——

我将放弃所有伪辞和自怜之情——

而诗歌鼓励我并擦拭我额头。

如今他们会说我竟咬那喂我的手。

歌唱学院

我的灵魂有美妙的播种季节，
大自然的秀美与恐怖共同育我
长成：它们偏爱我——在我的出生地，
也在不久后我迁居的那可爱的
山谷……

威廉·华兹华斯，《序曲》①

他［小马倌］有一本奥兰治歌谣集，我们在干草棚里一起读这些歌谣的日子带给我最初的诗韵快乐。后来，我记得人们告诉我，有传言说芬尼亚共和兄弟会要发动起义、步枪正被分发给奥兰治党：当时，我刚开始梦想我未来的人生，我想我愿意同芬尼亚派战斗而死。

叶芝，《自传》

---

① 见威廉·华兹华斯《序曲，或一位诗人心灵的成长》（丁宏为译，北京大学出版社，2017年）。此段引文根据希尼这组诗歌的语境稍有改动。

1. 恐怖统治

给谢默斯·迪恩

嗯，如卡瓦纳所说，我们生活在

重要之地。圣科伦姆学院

孤独的陡坡，我曾在那里寄居

六载，俯瞰你的沼泽区。

我凝望那些新世界：布兰迪韦尔

灼烧的咽喉，泛光灯照亮的赛狗跑道，

电兔①的油门。第一个星期

我因为太想家，甚至吃不下

安抚我流亡生活的饼干。

一天晚上我把它们扔到栅栏外，

那是一九五一年九月，

莱基路上万家灯火，

雾中呈现琥珀色。一种暗中的

行为。

　　　　　然后是贝尔法斯特，然后伯克利。

两个人都变得更成熟，

游心诗海直至诗歌成为

生命：从那些假期抵达的

———————————

① 用来刺激赛狗的兔形装置。

大信封到题写着"作者敬赠"

寄来的一本本薄诗集。

那些手写的诗，从你的线圈

练习本撕下来，让我着迷——

元音和思想自由放飞

像种球飘落于我们的梧桐。

我尝试写一写梧桐

并发明了一种南部德里韵

用 *hushed* 与 *lulled* 完美应和 *pushed* 与 *pulled*。

那些来自山那边的马丁靴

正踏遍，天啊，所有上好的

言辞的草坪。

我们的口音

变了吗？"总的来说，天主教徒不如

新教学校的学生口语好。"

还记得那些事吗？那些自卑

情结，那些造梦的材料。

"你叫什么名字，希尼？"

                    "希尼，神父。"

                            "很
好。"

    在我入学第一天，皮带

在校长办公室里发飙，

回声啪啪响在我们垂头的上空，

但我依然给家里写信说，寄宿生的日子

没那么糟，一如既往地避而不谈。

然后，在悠长的假期，我复活

在奥斯汀十六型的亲吻椅上，

车停在山墙下，发动机运转，

我的手指像常春藤贴紧她的肩，

厨房里有一盏灯为她点燃。

然后朝着回家的方向走，夏日的

自由夜复一夜地递减，空气里

全是月光和干草的芳香，警察

挥舞他们猩红的闪光灯，围住

汽车像黑黢黢的牲畜，大声嗅探并把

轻机枪的枪口对准我的眼睛：

"你叫什么名字，司机？"

> "谢默斯……"

> "谢默斯？"

他们曾在关卡读我的信

并用手电筒照你的象形文，

字迹精细的"优雅措辞"。

阿尔斯特是英国的，但无权过问
英语抒情诗：在我们周围，尽管
未曾命名，尽是恐怖统治。

2.警察来访

他的自行车停在窗台下，
防溅器的橡胶罩
环绕前轮挡泥板，
胖胖的黑把手

在阳光下发烫，"土豆"状的
电机闪烁并向后扳起，
脚蹬悬空，卸下了
法律的皮靴。

他的帽子倒过来
放在地板上，在他椅子旁。
帽子的压痕像一条斜边
分割他微微汗湿的头发。

他解开大账本的
带子，我父亲便
用亩、路得和杆①
来计算耕地收益。

---

①路得（rood）、杆（perch）都是英国中古时期丈量土地面积的
单位。

算术和恐惧。
我坐着注视那锃亮的枪套，
盖子扣着，编织的穗带
缠绕枪托。

"还有其他根茎作物吗？
甜菜，甘蓝，诸如此类？"
"没有。"但土豆田里
没有播种的地方

不是有一排芜菁吗？我感到
小小的罪过并坐在那儿
想象营房的黑洞。
他起身，移了移

他皮带上的警棍套，
合上末日审判簿，
双手把帽子戴好，
边道别边望着我。

一个影子在窗口颠簸。
他啪嗒一声用车尾架的弹簧
压住账本。他的靴子一撑，
自行车嘀嗒，嘀嗒，嘀嗒。

3. 奥兰治鼓，蒂龙，一九六六年

兰贝鼓在他的肚皮鼓起，向后
压在他的腰身，将万钧雷霆
完全安放在下巴和双膝之间。
那把他压垮的东西将他抬升。

每条胳膊都被老练的鼓槌延伸，
而他招摇其后。尽管鼓手
获准穿过点头赞许的人群，
其实是鼓在主宰，如巨大的肿瘤。

每一只耳朵都竖起，如同饕餮，
他猛击的信号曲奏响"不要教皇"。
山羊皮有时布满他的血。
空气如听诊器砰砰作响。

4. 一九六九年夏

当警察部队用枪瞄准暴民
向福尔斯路开火，我只是在
忍受马德里肆虐的骄阳。
每天下午，在寓所慢炖的
灼热中，当我汗流浃背地
苦读乔伊斯的人生，渔市的腥味
飘来如同亚麻池的臭气。
夜晚的阳台上，葡萄酒的纹章红，
黑暗的角落里似有孩童，
敞开的窗前披黑纱的老妇，
空气是流淌着西班牙语的峡谷。
我们在星光下的平原上聊天回家，
国民卫队的漆皮在黑暗中闪烁
如被亚麻污染的水塘里的鱼肚。

"回去，"一个说，"尝试接触人民。"
另一个从山中召来洛尔迦的亡魂。
我们熬过电视播报的死亡人数
和斗牛赛讯，名人们从那真实事件
仍在发生之地陆续抵达。

我回到普拉多美术馆的阴凉。
戈雅的《五月三日的枪决》
覆盖整面墙——起义者举起的
手臂和痉挛，戴头盔和
背行囊的武装部队，机枪扫射的
有效角度。在隔壁展厅，
他的噩梦，被嫁接在宫墙——
黑暗的气旋，集结，溃散；农神
被他自己孩子的鲜血装点；
巨神**混沌**将他野蛮的屁股
转向世人。以及，那场决斗，
两个狂徒为了荣誉用棍棒
打死对方，陷入沼泽，沉溺。

当历史袭来，他拳肘交加地作画，
挥舞他心灵的血染披风。

5. 领 养

给迈克尔·麦克莱弗蒂[①]

"描述即启示。"皇家

大道，贝尔法斯特，一九六二年，

一个星期六的下午，很高兴见到

我，语言的学徒，他握紧

我的手臂。"听着。走你自己的路。

做你自己的事。记住

凯瑟琳·曼斯菲尔德——我将描述

洗衣篮怎样尖叫……那被放逐的音调。"

让夸大其词见鬼去吧：

"别让血管在你的圆珠笔里膨胀。"

然后说，"可怜的霍普金斯！"我有他赠我的

《日记》，划了着重线，他被压垮的自我

俯首日记中的苦痛。他能

处处明辨耐心的轮廓，

领养我又送出我，他的文字

压在我舌上如奥波勒斯古币。

---

① 迈克尔·麦克莱弗蒂（Micael McLaverty，1904–1992），爱尔兰短篇小说家。

6. 曝 光

此刻是十二月的威克洛：
赤杨滴沥，白桦
承继最后的光，
梣树看着都冷。

迷途的彗星
会在日落时显现，
那数百万吨的光
只如山楂和玫瑰果一闪，

而我有时看到一颗坠落的星辰。
若我能乘流星的辉光而来该多好！
相反我走在潮湿的落叶间，
还有空壳，枯竭的秋虫，

想象一位英雄
在某处泥泞的围场，
其天赋如掷出的石弹
为绝望者飞旋。

我怎么竟成了现在的样子？

我常常想起朋友们

棱镜般美妙的建议

和那些恨我者的铁脑

当我坐在那里再三掂量

我那负责任的悲伤。

为了什么？为耳朵？为了人民？

为了背后的议论？

雨落在赤杨间，

它宜人的低音

低语失望和损蚀

而每一滴都使人忆起

钻石的绝对。

我不是拘留犯亦非告密者；

一个内在的流亡者，蓄长发 ①

而多虑；一个藏身林中的步兵

逃过了那场大屠杀，

利用树干和树皮织成

---

① 蓄长发（long-haired），也指具有文人气的。该表述与音乐有关，尤其指爱听古典音乐的知识分子。

自我保护的颜色，感受
各个方向疾风的劲吹；

他吹扬这些火花
获取微薄的温暖，错失
一生只有一次的征兆，
彗星搏动的玫瑰。

希尼肖像，Edward McGuire 绘，一九七三至一九七四年（北爱尔兰国家博物馆）。希尼在《一篮栗子》里追忆了画家为诗人画像的情景，收录于《幻视》。

Wintering Out

For David Hammond and Michael Longley

This morning from a dewy motorway
I saw the new camp for the internees:
a bomb had left a crater of fresh clay
in the roadside, and over in the trees

machine-gun posts defined a real stockade.
There was that white mist you get on a low ground
and it was déjà-vu, some film made
of Stalag 17, a bad dream with no sound.

Is there a life before death? That's chalked up
on a wall downtown. Competence with pain,
coherent miseries, a bite and sup,
we hug our little destiny again.

Contents

Acknowledgements and Notes

Acknowledgements are due to the editors of the following magazines where most of these poems appeared, a number of them in slightly different form:

Aquarius, Atlantis, Criterion (Galway), *The Critical Quarterly, Gown, The Guardian, Hibernia, Honest Ulsterman, Irish Press, Irish Times, Listener, The Malahat Review, Michigan Quarterly Review, New Statesman, Occident, Phoenix, Poetry* (Chicago), *Poetry Book Society Supplement, Stand, Threshold*; and to the editor of *Modern Poets in Focus* 2 (Corgi) and *The Young British Poets* (Chatto).

'Fireside' and Sections II and V of 'Summer Home' (originally entitled 'Home' and 'Aubade') © *The New Yorker*, 1971.

'Land', 'Servant Boy' and Sections III and IV of 'Summer Home' appeared as broadsheets from Poem of the Month, The Red Hanrahan Press and Tara Telephone respectively.

'Bye-Child' appeared in *Twelve to Twelve* (Camden Festival, 1970); 'Servant Boy' appeared in *Responses* (National Book League and Poetry Society, 1971).

'The Tollund Man' and 'Nerthus' originated from a reading of P. V. Glob's *The Bog People* (Faber).

'Maighdean Mara' is the Irish for 'mermaid'.

PART ONE

Fodder

Or, as we said,
fother, I open
my arms for it
again. But first

to draw from the tight
vise of a stack
the weathered eaves
of the stack itself

falling at your feet,
last summer's tumbled
swathes of grass
and meadowsweet

multiple as loaves
and fishes, a bundle
tossed over half-doors
or into mucky gaps.

These long nights
I would pull hay
for comfort, anything
to bed the stall.

Bog Oak

A carter's trophy
Split for rafters,
a cobwebbed, black,
long-seasoned rib

under the first thatch.
I might tarry
with the moustached
dead, the creel-fillers,

or eavesdrop on
their hopeless wisdom
as a blow-down of smoke
struggles over the half-door

and mizzling rain
blurs the far end
of the cart track.
The softening ruts

lead back to no
'oak groves', no
cutters of mistletoe
in the green clearings.

Perhaps I just make out
Edmund Spenser,
dreaming sunlight,
encroached upon by

geniuses who creep
'out of every corner
of the woodes and glennes'
towards watercress and carrion.

Anahorish

My 'place of clear water',
the first hill in the world
where springs washed into
the shiny grass

and darkened cobbles
in the bed of the lane.
Anahorish, soft gradient
of consonant, vowel-meadow,

after-image of lamps
swung through the yards
on winter evenings.
With pails and barrows

those mound-dwellers
go waist-deep in mist
to break the light ice
at wells and dunghills.

Servant Boy

He is wintering out
the back-end of a bad year,
swinging a hurricane-lamp
through some outhouse;

a jobber among shadows.
Old work-whore, slave-
blood, who stepped fair-hills
under each bidder's eye

and kept your patience
and your counsel, how
you draw me into
your trail. Your trail

broken from haggard to stable,
a straggle of fodder
stiffened on snow,
comes first-footing

the back doors of the little
barons: resentful
and impenitent,
carrying the warm eggs.

The Last Mummer

I

Carries a stone in his pocket,
an ash-plant under his arm.

Moves out of the fog
on the lawn, pads up the terrace.

The luminous screen in the corner
has them charmed in a ring

so he stands a long time behind them.
St. George, Beelzebub and Jack Straw

can't be conjured from mist.
He catches the stick in his fist

and, shrouded, starts beating
the bars of the gate.

His boots crack the road. The stone
clatters down off the slates.

II

He came trammelled
in the taboos of the country

picking a nice way through
the long toils of blood

and feuding.
His tongue went whoring

among the civil tongues,

he had an eye for weather-eyes

at cross-roads and lane-ends
and could don manners

at a flutter of curtains.
His straw mask and hunch were fabulous

disappearing beyond the lamplit
slabs of a yard.

III

You dream a cricket in the hearth
and cockroach on the floor,

a line of mummers
marching out the door

as the lamp flares in the draught.
Melted snow off their feet

leaves you in peace.
Again an old year dies

on your hearthstone, for good luck.
The moon's host elevated

in a monstrance of holly trees,
he makes dark tracks, who had

untousled a first dewy path
into the summer grazing.

Land

I

I stepped it, perch by perch.
Unbraiding rushes and grass
I opened my right-of-way
through old bottoms and sowed-out ground
and gathered stones off the ploughing
to raise a small cairn.
Cleaned out the drains, faced the hedges
often got up at dawn
to walk the outlying fields.

I composed habits for those acres
so that my last look would be
neither gluttonous nor starved.
I was ready to go anywhere.

II

This is in place of what I would leave
plaited and branchy
on a long slope of stubble:

a woman of old wet leaves,
rush-bands and thatcher's scollops,
stooked loosely, her breasts an open-work

of new straw and harvest bows.
Gazing out past
the shifting hares.

III

I sense the pads
unfurling under grass and clover:

if I lie with my ear
in this loop of silence

long enough, thigh-bone
and shoulder against the phantom ground,

I expect to pick up
a small drumming

and must not be surprised
in bursting air

to find myself snared, swinging
an ear-ring of sharp wire.

Gifts of Rain

I

Cloudburst and steady downpour now
for days.
        Still mammal,
straw-footed on the mud,
he begins to sense weather
by his skin.

A nimble snout of flood
licks over stepping stones
and goes uprooting.
            He fords
his life by sounding.
              Soundings.

II

A man wading lost fields
 breaks the pane of flood:

a flower of mud-
water blooms up to his reflection

like a cut swaying
its red spoors through a basin.

His hands grub
where the spade has uncastled

sunken drills, an atlantis
he depends on. So

he is hooped to where he planted
and sky and ground

are running naturally among his arms
that grope the cropping land.

III

When rains were gathering
there would be an all-night
roaring off the ford.
Their world-schooled ear

could monitor the usual
confabulations, the race
slabbering past the gable,
the Moyola harping on

its gravel beds:
all spouts by daylight
brimmed with their own airs
and overflowed each barrel

in long tresses.
I cock my ear
at an absence –
in the shared calling of blood

arrives my need
for antediluvian lore.
Soft voices of the dead
are whispering by the shore

that I would question
(and for my children's sake)
about crops rotted, river mud
glazing the baked clay floor.

IV

The tawny guttural water
spells itself: Moyola
is its own score and consort,

bedding the locale
in the utterance,
reed music, an old chanter

breathing its mists
through vowels and history.
A swollen river,

a mating call of sound
rises to pleasure me, Dives,
hoarder of common ground.

Toome

My mouth holds round
the soft blastings,
Toome, Toome,
as under the dislodged

slab of the tongue
I push into a souterrain
prospecting what new
in a hundred centuries'

loam, flints, musket-balls,
fragmented ware,
torcs and fish-bones
till I am sleeved in

alluvial mud that shelves
suddenly under
bogwater and tributaries,
and elvers tail my hair.

Broagh

Riverback, the long rigs
ending in broad docken
and a canopied pad
down to the ford.

The garden mould
bruised easily, the shower
gathering in your heelmark
was the black *O*

in *Broagh*,
its low tattoo
among the windy boortrees
and rhubarb-blades

ended almost
suddenly, like that last
gh the strangers found
difficult to manage.

Oracle

Hide in the hollow trunk
of the willow tree,
its listening familiar,
until, as usual, they
cuckoo your name
across the fields.
You can hear them
draw the poles of stiles
as they approach
calling you out:
small mouth and ear
in a woody cleft,
lobe and larynx
of the mossy places.

The Backward Look

A stagger in air
as if a language
failed, a sleight
of wing.

A snipe's bleat is fleeing
its nesting ground
into dialect,
into variants,

transliterations whirr
on the nature reserves –
little goat of the air,
of the evening,

little goat of the frost.
It is his tail-feathers
drumming elegies
in the slipstream

of wild goose
and yellow bittern
as he corkscrews away
into the vaults

that we live off, his flight
through the sniper's eyrie,
over twilit earthworks
and wall-steads,

disappearing among
gleanings and leavings
in the combs
of a fieldworker's archive.

Traditions

For Tom Flanagan

I

Our guttural muse
was bulled long ago
by the alliterative tradition,
her uvula grows

vestigial, forgotten
like the coccyx
or a Brigid's Cross
yellowing in some outhouse

while custom, that 'most
sovereign mistress',
beds us down into
the British isles.

II

We are to be proud
of our Elizabethan English:
'varsity', for example,
is grass-roots stuff with us;

we 'deem' or we 'allow'
when we suppose
and some cherished archaisms
are correct Shakespearean.

Not to speak of the furled
consonants of lowlanders
shuttling obstinately
between bawn and mossland.

III

MacMorris, gallivanting
round the Globe, whinged
to courtier and groundling
who had heard tell of us

as going very bare
of learning, as wild hares,
as anatomies of death:
'What ish my nation?'

And sensibly, though so much
later, the wandering Bloom
replied, 'Ireland,' said Bloom,
'I was born here. Ireland.'

A New Song

I met a girl from Derrygarve
And the name, a lost potent musk,
Recalled the river's long swerve,
A kingfisher's blue bolt at dusk

And stepping stones like black molars
Sunk in the ford, the shifty glaze
Of the whirlpool, the Moyola
Pleasuring beneath alder trees.

And Derrygarve, I thought, was just,
Vanished music, twilit water,
A smooth libation of the past
Poured by this chance vestal daughter.

But now our river tongues must rise
From licking deep in native haunts
To flood, with vowelling embrace,
Demesnes staked out in consonants.

And Castledawson we'll enlist
And Upperlands, each planted bawn –
Like bleaching-greens resumed by grass –
A vocable, as rath and bullaun.

The Other Side

I

Thigh-deep in sedge and marigolds
a neighbour laid his shadow
on the stream, vouching

'It's poor as Lazarus, that ground,'
and brushed away
among the shaken leafage:

I lay where his lea sloped
to meet our fallow,
nested on moss and rushes,

my ear swallowing
his fabulous, biblical dismissal,
that tongue of chosen people.

When he would stand like that
on the other side, white-haired,
swinging his blackthorn

at the marsh weeds,
he prophesied above our scraggy acres,
then turned away

towards his promised furrows
on the hill, a wake of pollen
drifting to our bank, next season's tares.

II

For days we would rehearse
each patriarchal dictum:
Lazarus, the Pharaoh, Solomon

and David and Goliath rolled
magnificently, like loads of hay
too big for our small lanes,

or faltered on a rut –
'Your side of the house, I believe,
hardly rule by the book at all.'

His brain was a whitewashed kitchen
hung with texts, swept tidy
as the body o' the kirk.

III

Then sometimes when the rosary was dragging
mournfully on in the kitchen
we would hear his step round the gable

though not until after the litany
would the knock come to the door
and the casual whistle strike up

on the doorstep. 'A right-looking night,'
he might say, 'I was dandering by
and says I, I might as well call.'

But now I stand behind him
in the dark yard, in the moan of prayers.
He puts a hand in a pocket

or taps a little tune with the blackthorn
shyly, as if he were party to
lovemaking or a stranger's weeping.

Should I slip away, I wonder,
or go up and touch his shoulder
and talk about the weather

or the price of grass-seed?

The Wool Trade

'How different are the words "home",
"Christ", "ale", "master", on his
lips and on mine.' STEPHEN DEDALUS

'The wool trade' – the phrase
Rambled warm as a fleece

Out of his hoard.
To shear, to bale and bleach and card

Unwound from the spools
Of his vowels

And square-set men in tunics
Who plied soft names like Bruges

In their talk, merchants
Back from the Netherlands:

O all the hamlets where
Hills and flocks and streams conspired

To a language of waterwheels,
A lost syntax of looms and spindles,

How they hang
Fading, in the gallery of the tongue!

And I must talk of tweed,
A stiff cloth with flecks like blood.

Linen Town

High Street, Belfast, 1786

It's twenty to four
By the public clock. A cloaked rider
Clops off into an entry

Coming perhaps from the Linen Hall
Or Cornmarket
Where, the civic print unfrozen,

In twelve years' time
They hanged young McCracken –
This lownecked belle and tricorned fop's

Still flourish undisturbed
By the swinging tongue of his body.
Pen and ink, water tint

Fence and fetch us in
Under bracketed tavern signs,
The edged gloom of arcades.

It's twenty to four
On one of the last afternoons
Of reasonable light.

Smell the tidal Lagan:
Take a last turn
In the tang of possibility.

A Northern Hoard

And some in dreams assured were
Of the Spirit that plagued us so

1. *Roots*

Leaf membranes lid the window.
In the streetlamp's glow
Your body's moonstruck
To drifted barrow, sunk glacial rock.

And all shifts dreamily as you keen
Far off, turning from the din
Of gunshot, siren and clucking gas
Out there beyond each curtained terrace

Where the fault is opening. The touch of love,
Your warmth heaving to the first move,
Grows helpless in our old Gomorrah.
We petrify or uproot now.

I'll dream it for us before dawn
When the pale sniper steps down
And I approach the shrub.
I've soaked by moonlight in tidal blood

A mandrake, lodged human fork,
Earth sac, limb of the dark;
And I wound its damp smelly loam
And stop my ears against the scream.

2. *No Man's Land*

I deserted, shut out
their wounds' fierce awning,
those palms like streaming webs.

Must I crawl back now,
spirochete, abroad between
shred-hung wire and thorn,
to confront my smeared doorstep
and what lumpy dead?
Why do I unceasingly
arrive late to condone
infected sutures
and ill-knit bone?

3. *Stump*

I am riding to plague again.
Sometimes under a sooty wash
From the grate in the burnt-out gable
I see the needy in a small pow-wow.
What do I say if they wheel out their dead?
I'm cauterized, a black stump of home.

4. *No Sanctuary*

It's Hallowe'en. The turnip-man's lopped head
Blazes at us through split bottle glass
And fumes and swims up like a wrecker's lantern.

Death mask of harvest, mocker at All Souls
With scorching smells, red dog's eyes in the night –
We ring and stare into unhallowed light.

5. *Tinder*

We picked flints,
Pale and dirt-veined,

So small finger and thumb
Ached around them;

Cold beads of history and home
We fingered, a cave-mouth flame

Of leaf and stick
Trembling at the mind's wick.

We clicked stone on stone
That sparked a weak flame-pollen

And failed, our knuckle joints
Striking as often as the flints.

What did we know then
Of tinder, charred linen and iron,

Huddled at dusk in a ring,
Our fists shut, our hope shrunken?

What could strike a blaze
From our dead igneous days?

Now we squat on cold cinder,
Red-eyed, after the flames' soft thunder

And our thoughts settle like ash.
We face the tundra's whistling brush

With new history, flint and iron,
Cast-offs, scraps, nail, canine.

Midnight

Since the professional wars –
Corpse and carrion
Paling in rain –
The wolf has died out

In Ireland. The packs
Scoured parkland and moor
Till a Quaker buck and his dogs
Killed the last one

In some scraggy waste of Kildare.
The wolfhound was crossed
With inferior strains,
Forests coopered to wine casks.

Rain on the roof to-night
Sogs turf-banks and heather,
Sets glinting outcrops
Of basalt and granite,

Drips to the moss of bare boughs.
The old dens are soaking.
The pads are lost or
Retrieved by small vermin

That glisten and scut.
Nothing is panting, lolling,
Vapouring. The tongue's
Leashed in my throat.

The Tollund Man

I

Some day I will go to Aarhus
To see his peat-brown head,
The mild pods of his eye-lids,
His pointed skin cap.

In the flat country nearby
Where they dug him out,
His last gruel of winter seeds
Caked in his stomach,

Naked except for
The cap, noose and girdle,
I will stand a long time.
Bridegroom to the goddess,

She tightened her torc on him
And opened her fen,
Those dark juices working
Him to a saint's kept body,

Trove of the turfcutters'
Honeycombed workings.
Now his stained face
Reposes at Aarhus.

II

I could risk blasphemy,
Consecrate the cauldron bog
Our holy ground and pray
Him to make germinate

The scattered, ambushed

Flesh of labourers,
Stockinged corpses
Laid out in the farmyards,

Tell-tale skin and teeth
Flecking the sleepers
Of four young brothers, trailed
For miles along the lines.

III

Something of his sad freedom
As he rode the tumbril
Should come to me, driving,
Saying the names

Tollund, Grabaulle, Nebelgard,
Watching the pointing hands
Of country people,
Not knowing their tongue.

Out there in Jutland
In the old man-killing parishes
I will feel lost,
Unhappy and at home.

Nerthus

For beauty, say an ash-fork staked in peat,
Its long grains gathering to the gouged split;

A seasoned, unsleeved taker of the weather,
Where kesh and loaning finger out to heather.

Cairn-maker

For Barrie Cooke

He robbed the stones' nests, uncradled
As he orphaned and betrothed rock
To rock: his unaccustomed hand
Went chambering upon hillock

And bogland. Clamping, balancing,
That whole day spent in the Burren,
He did not find and add to them
But piled up small cairn after cairn

And dressed some stones with his own mark.
Which he tells of with almost fear;
And of strange affiliation
To what was touched and handled there,

Unexpected hives and castlings
Pennanted now, claimed by no hand:
Rush and ladysmock, heather-bells
Blowing in each aftermath of wind.

Navvy

The moleskins stiff as bark,
the drill grafting his wrists
to the shale:
where the surface is weavy

and the camber tilts
in the slow lane, he stands
waving you down. The morass
the macadam snakes over

swallowed his yellow bulldozer
four years ago, laying it down
with lake-dwellings and dug-outs,
pike-shafts, axe-heads, bone pins,

all he is indifferent to.
He has not relented
under weather or insults,
my brother and keeper

plugged to the hard-core,
picking along
the welted, stretchmarked
curve of the world.

Veteran's Dream

Mr Dickson, my neighbour,
Who saw the last cavalry charge
Of the war and got the first gas
Walks with a limp

Into his helmet and khaki.
He notices indifferently
The gas has yellowed his buttons
And near his head

Horses plant their shods.
His real fear is gangrene.
He wakes with his hand to the scar
And they do their white magic

Where he lies
On cankered ground,
A scatter of maggots, busy
In the trench of his wound.

Augury

The fish faced into the current,
Its mouth agape,
Its whole head opened like a valve.
You said 'It's diseased.'

A pale crusted sore
Turned like a coin
And wound to the bottom,
Unsettling silt off a weed.

We hang charmed
On the trembling catwalk:
What can fend us now
Can soothe the hurt eye

Of the sun,
Unpoison great lakes,
Turn back
The rat on the road.

PART TWO

Wedding Day

I am afraid.
Sound has stopped in the day
And the images reel over
And over. Why all those tears,

The wild grief on his face
Outside the taxi? The sap
Of mourning rises
In our waving guests.

You sing behind the tall cake
Like a deserted bride
Who persists, demented,
And goes through the ritual.

When I went to the gents
There was a skewered heart
And a legend of love. Let me
sleep on your breast to the airport.

Mother of the Groom

What she remembers
Is his glistening back
In the bath, his small boots
In the ring of boots at her feet.

Hands in her voided lap,
She hears a daughter welcomed.
It's as if he kicked when lifted
And slipped her soapy hold.

Once soap would ease off
The wedding ring
That's bedded forever now
In her clapping hand.

Summer Home

I

Was it wind off the dumps
or something in heat

dogging us, the summer gone sour,
a fouled nest incubating somewhere?

Whose fault, I wondered, inquisitor
of the possessed air.

To realize suddenly,
whip off the mat

that was larval, moving –
and scald, scald, scald.

II

Bushing the door, my arms full
of wild cherry and rhododendron,
I hear her small lost weeping
through the hall, that bells and hoarsens
on my name, my name.

O love, here is the blame.

The loosened flowers between us
gather in, compose
for a May altar of sorts.
These frank and falling blooms
soon taint to a sweet chrism.

Attend. Anoint the wound.

III

O we tented our wound all right
under the homely sheet

and lay as if the cold flat of a blade
had winded us.

More and more I postulate
thick healings, like now

as you bend in the shower
water lives down the tilting stoups of your breasts.

IV

With a final
unmusical drive
long grains begin
to open and split

ahead and once more
we sap
the white, trodden
path to the heart.

V

My children weep out the hot foreign night.
We walk the floor, my foul mouth takes it out
On you and we lie stiff till dawn
Attends the pillow, and the maize, and vine

That holds its filling burden to the light.
Yesterday rocks sang when we tapped
Stalactites in the cave's old, dripping dark –
Our love calls tiny as a tuning fork.

Serenades

The Irish nightingale
Is a sedge-warbler,
A little bird with a big voice
Kicking up a racket all night.

Not what you'd expect
From the musical nation.
I haven't even heard one –
Nor an owl, for that matter.

My serenades have been
The broken voice of a crow
In a draught or a dream,
The wheeze of bats

Or the ack-ack
Of the tramp corncrake
Lost in a no man's land
Between combines and chemicals.

So fill the bottles, love,
Leave them inside their cots.
And if they do wake us, well,
So would the sedge-warbler.

Somnambulist

Nestrobber's hands
and a face in its net of gossamer;

he came back weeping
to unstarch the pillow

and freckle her sheets
with tiny yolk.

A Winter's Tale

A pallor in the headlights'
Range wavered and disappeared.
Weeping, blood bright from her cuts
Where she'd fled the hedged and wired
Road, they eyed her nakedness
Astray among the cattle
At first light. Lanterns, torches
And the searchers' gay babble
She eluded earlier:
Now her own people only
Closed around her dazed whimper
With rugs, dressings and brandy –
Conveying maiden daughter
Back to family hearth and floor.
Why run, our lovely daughter,
Bare-breasted from our door?

Still, like good luck, she returned.
Some nights, crossing the thresholds
Of empty homes, she warmed
Her dewy roundings and folds
To sleep in the chimney nook.
After all, they were neighbours.
As neighbours, when they came back
Surprised but unmalicious
Greetings passed
Between them. She was there first
And so appeared no haunter
But, making all comers guests,
She stirred as from a winter
Sleep. Smiled. Uncradled her breasts.

Shore Woman

Man to the hills, woman to the shore.
                                    Gaelic proverb

I have crossed the dunes with their whistling bent
Where dry loose sand was riddling round the air
And I'm walking the firm margin. White pocks
Of cockle, blanched roofs of clam and oyster
Hoard the moonlight, woven and unwoven
Off the bay. At the far rocks
A pale sud comes and goes.

Under boards the mackerel slapped to death
Yet still we took them in at every cast,
Stiff flails of cold convulsed with their first breath.
My line plumbed certainly the undertow,
Loaded against me once I went to draw
And flashed and fattened up towards the light.
He was all business in the stern. I called
'This is so easy that it's hardly right,'
But he unhooked and coped with frantic fish
Without speaking. Then suddenly it lulled,
We'd crossed where they were running, the line rose
Like a let-down and I was conscious
How far we'd drifted out beyond the head.
'Count them up at your end,' was all he said
Before I saw the porpoises' thick backs
Cartwheeling like the flywheels of the tide,
Soapy and shining. To have seen a hill
Splitting the water could not have numbed me more
Than the close irruption of that school,
Tight viscous muscle, hooped from tail to snout,
Each one revealed complete as it bowled out
And under.
                    They will attack a boat.
I knew it and I asked him to put in
But he would not, declared it was a yarn

My people had been fooled by far too long
And he would prove it now and settle it.
Maybe he shrank when those sloped oily backs
Propelled towards us: I lay and screamed
Under splashed brine in an open rocking boat
Feeling each dunt and slither through the timber,
Sick at their huge pleasures in the water.

I sometimes walk this strand for thanksgiving
Or maybe it's to get away from him
Skittering his spit across the stove. Here
Is the taste of safety, the shelving sand
Harbours no worse than razor-shell or crab –
Though my father recalls carcasses of whales
Collapsed and gasping, right up to the dunes.
But to-night such moving sinewed dreams lie out
In darker fathoms, far beyond the head.
Astray upon a debris of scrubbed shells
Between parched dunes and salivating wave,
I have rights on this fallow avenue,
A membrane between moonlight and my shadow.

Maighdean Mara

For Seán Oh-Eocha

I

She sleeps now, her cold breasts
Dandled by undertow,
Her hair lifted and laid.
Undulant slow seawracks
Cast about shin and thigh,
Bangles of wort, drifting
Liens catch, dislodge gently.

This is the great first sleep
Of homecoming, eight
Land years between hearth and
Bed steeped and dishevelled.
Her magic garment al-
most ocean-tinctured still.

II

He stole her garments as
She combed her hair: follow
Was all that she could do.
He hid it in the eaves
And charmed her there, four walls,
Warm floor, man-love nightly
In earshot of the waves.

She suffered milk and birth –
She had no choice – conjured
Patterns of home and drained
The tidesong from her voice.
Then the thatcher came and stuck
Her garment in a stack.
Children carried tales back.

III

In night air, entering
Foam, she wrapped herself
With smoke-reeks from his thatch,
Straw-musts and films of mildew.
She dipped his secret there
Forever and uncharmed

Accents of fisher wives,
The dead hold of bedrooms,
Dread of the night and morrow,
Her children's brush and combs.
She sleeps now, her cold breasts
Dandled by undertow.

Limbo

Fishermen at Ballyshannon
Netted an infant last night
Along with the salmon.
An illegitimate spawning,

A small one thrown back
To the waters. But I'm sure
As she stood in the shallows
Ducking him tenderly

Till the frozen knobs of her wrists
Were dead as the gravel,
He was a minnow with hooks
Tearing her open.

She waded in under
The sign of her cross.
He was hauled in with the fish.
Now limbo will be

A cold glitter of souls
Through some far briny zone.
Even Christ's palms, unhealed,
Smart and cannot fish there.

Bye-Child

He was discovered in the henhouse
where she had confined him. He was
incapable of saying anything.

When the lamp glowed,
A yolk of light
In their back window,
The child in the outhouse
Put his eye to a chink –

Little henhouse boy,
Sharp-faced as new moons
Remembered, your photo still
Glimpsed like a rodent
On the floor of my mind,

Little moon man,
Kennelled and faithful
At the foot of the yard,
Your frail shape, luminous,
Weightless, is stirring the dust,

The cobwebs, old droppings
Under the roosts
And dry smells from scraps
She put through your trapdoor
Morning and evening.

After those footsteps, silence;
Vigils, solitudes, fasts,
Unchristened tears,
A puzzled love of the light.
But now you speak at last

With a remote mime
Of something beyond patience,

Your gaping wordless proof
Of lunar distances
Travelled beyond love.

Good-night

A latch lifting, an edged den of light
Opens across the yard. Out of the low door
They stoop into the honeyed corridor,
Then walk straight through the wall of the dark.

A puddle, cobble-stones, jambs and doorstep
Are set steady in a block of brightness.
Till she strides in again beyond her shadows
And cancels everything behind her.

First Calf

It's a long time since I saw
The afterbirth strung on the hedge
As if the wind smarted
And streamed bloodshot tears.

Somewhere about the cow stands
With her head almost outweighing
Her tense sloped neck,
The calf hard at her udder.

The shallow bowls of her eyes
Tilt membrane and fluid.
The warm plaque of her snout gathers
A growth round moist nostrils.

Her hide stays warm in the wind.
Her wide eyes read nothing.
The semaphores of hurt
Swaddle and flap on a bush.

May

When I looked down from the bridge
Trout were flipping the sky
Into smithereens, the stones
Of the wall warmed me.

Wading green stems, lugs of leaf
That untangle and bruise
(Their tiny gushers of juice)
My toecaps sparkle now

Over the soft fontanel
Of Ireland. I should wear
Hide shoes, the hair next my skin,
For walking this ground:

Wasn't there a spa-well,
Its coping grassy, pendent?
And then the spring issuing
Right across the tarmac.

I'm out to find that village,
Its low sills fragrant
With ladysmock and celandine,
Marshlights in the summer dark.

Fireside

Always there would be stories of lights
hovering among bushes or at the foot
of a meadow; maybe a goat with cold horns
pluming into the moon; a tingle of chains

on the midnight road. And then maybe
word would come round of that watery
art, the lamping of fishes, and I'd be
mooning my flashlamp on the licked black pelt

of the stream, my left arm splayed to take
a heavy pour and run of the current
occluding the net. Was that the beam
buckling over an eddy or a gleam

of the fabulous? Steady the light
and come to your senses, they're saying good-night.

Dawn

Somebody lets up a blind.
The shrub at the window
Glitters, a mint of green leaves
Pitched and tossed.

When we stopped for lights
In the centre, pigeons were down
On the street, a scatter
Of cobbles, clucking and settling.

We went at five miles an hour.
A tut-tutting colloquy
Was in session, scholars
Arguing through until morning

In a Pompeian silence.
The dummies watched from the window
Displays as we slipped to the sea.
I got away out by myself

On a scurf of winkles and cockles
And found myself suddenly
Unable to move without crunching
Acres of their crisp delicate turrets.

Travel

Oxen supporting their heads
into the afternoon sun,
melons studding the hill like brass:

who reads into distances reads
beyond us, our sleeping children
and the dust settling in scorched grass.

Westering

In California

I sit under Rand McNally's
'Official Map of the Moon' –
The colour of frogskin,
Its enlarged pores held

Open and one called
'Pitiscus' at eye level –
Recalling the last night
In Donegal, my shadow

Neat upon the whitewash
From her bony shine,
The cobbles of the yard
Lit pale as eggs.

Summer had been a free fall
Ending there,
The empty amphitheatre
Of the west. Good Friday

We had started out
Past shopblinds drawn on the afternoon,
Cars stilled outside still churches,
Bikes tilting to a wall;

We drove by,
A dwindling interruption
As clappers smacked
On a bare altar

And congregations bent
To the studded crucifix.
What nails dropped out that hour?
Roads unreeled, unreeled

Falling light as casts
Laid down
On shining waters.
Under the moon's stigmata

Six thousand miles away,
I imagine untroubled dust,
A loosening gravity,
Christ weighing by his hands.

North

Contents

Acknowledgements

The author gratefully acknowledges the assistance of the American Irish Foundation during 1973/4 when he was recipient of their annual Literary Award.

Acknowledgements are due to the editors of the following where some of these poems appeared for the first time: *Antaeus*, *The Arts in Ireland*, *Causeway* (BBC Radio 3), *Encounter*, *Exile*, *Hibernia*, *The Irish Press*, *The Irish Times*, *Irish University Review*, *James Joyce Quarterly*, *The Listener*, *The New Review*, *Phoenix*, *The Times Literary Supplement*; and to the editors of the following anthologies: *The Faber Book of Irish Verse*, *New Poems 1972–1973* and *New Poems 1973–1974* (Hutchinson), and *Soundings '72* (Blackstaff, Belfast).

Eight of the poems appeared in a limited edition entitled *Bog Poems* (Rainbow Press).

Mossbawn: Two Poems in Dedication
for Mary Heaney

1. *Sunlight*

There was a sunlit absence.
The helmeted pump in the yard
heated its iron,
water honeyed

in the slung bucket
and the sun stood
like a griddle cooling
against the wall

of each long afternoon.
So, her hands scuffled
over the bakeboard,
the reddening stove

sent its plaque of heat
against her where she stood
in a floury apron
by the window.

Now she dusts the board
with a goose's wing,
now sits, broad-lapped,
with whitened nails

and measling shins:
here is a space
again, the scone rising
to the tick of two clocks.

And here is love

like a tinsmith's scoop
sunk past its gleam
in the meal-bin.

2. *The Seed Cutters*

They seem hundreds of years away. Breughel,
You'll know them if I can get them true.
They kneel under the hedge in a half-circle
Behind a windbreak wind is breaking through.
They are the seed cutters. The tuck and frill
Of leaf-sprout is on the seed potatoes
Buried under that straw. With time to kill,
They are taking their time. Each sharp knife goes
Lazily halving each root that falls apart
In the palm of the hand: a milky gleam,
And, at the centre, a dark watermark.
Oh, calendar customs! Under the broom
Yellowing over them, compose the frieze
With all of us there, our anonymities.

PART I

Antaeus

When I lie on the ground
I rise flushed as a rose in the morning.
In fights I arrange a fall on the ring
 To rub myself with sand

That is operative
As an elixir. I cannot be weaned
Off the earth's long contour, her river-veins.
 Down here in my cave,

Girded with root and rock,
I am cradled in the dark that wombed me
And nurtured in every artery
 Like a small hillock.

Let each new hero come
Seeking the golden apples and Atlas.
He must wrestle with me before he pass
 Into that realm of fame

Among sky-born and royal:
He may well throw me and renew my birth
But let him not plan, lifting me off the earth,
 My elevation, my fall.

1966

Belderg

'They just kept turning up
And were thought of as foreign' –
One-eyed and benign,
They lie about his house,
Quernstones out of a bog.

To lift the lid of the peat
And find this pupil dreaming
Of neolithic wheat!
When he stripped off blanket bog
The soft-piled centuries

Fell open like a glib:
There were the first plough-marks,
The stone-age fields, the tomb
Corbelled, turfed and chambered,
Floored with dry turf-coomb.

A landscape fossilized,
Its stone-wall patternings
Repeated before our eyes
In the stone walls of Mayo.
Before I turned to go

He talked about persistence,
A congruence of lives,
How, stubbed and cleared of stones,
His home accrued growth rings
Of iron, flint and bronze.

So I talked of Mossbawn,
A bogland name. 'But *moss*?'
He crossed my old home's music
With older strains of Norse.

I'd told how its foundation

Was mutable as sound
And how I could derive
A forked root from that ground,
Make *bawn* an English fort,
A planter's walled-in mound,

Or else find sanctuary
And think of it as Irish,
Persistent if outworn.
'But the Norse ring on your tree?'
I passed through the eye of the quern,

Grist to an ancient mill,
And in my mind's eye saw
A world-tree of balanced stones,
Querns piled like vertebrae,
The marrow crushed to grounds.

Funeral Rites

I shouldered a kind of manhood,
stepping in to lift the coffins
of dead relations.
They had been laid out

in tainted rooms,
their eyelids glistening,
their dough-white hands
shackled in rosary beads.

Their puffed knuckles
had unwrinkled, the nails
were darkened, the wrists
obediently sloped.

The dulse-brown shroud,
the quilted satin cribs:
I knelt courteously,
admiring it all,

as wax melted down
and veined the candles,
the flames hovering
to the women hovering

behind me.
And always, in a corner,
the coffin lid,
its nail-heads dressed

with little gleaming crosses.
Dear soapstone masks,
kissing their igloo brows

had to suffice

before the nails were sunk
and the black glacier
of each funeral
pushed away.

II

Now as news comes in
of each neighbourly murder
we pine for ceremony,
customary rhythms:

the temperate footsteps
of a cortège, winding past
each blinded home.
I would restore

the great chambers of Boyne,
prepare a sepulchre
under the cup-marked stones.
Out of side-streets and bye-roads

purring family cars
nose into line,
the whole country tunes
to the muffled drumming

of ten thousand engines.
Somnambulant women,
left behind, move
through emptied kitchens

imagining our slow triumph
towards the mounds.
Quiet as a serpent
in its grassy boulevard,

the procession drags its tail
out of the Gap of the North
as its head already enters
the megalithic doorway.

III

When they have put the stone
back in its mouth
we will drive north again
past Strang and Carling fjords,

the cud of memory
allayed for once, arbitration
of the feud placated,
imagining those under the hill

disposed like Gunnar
who lay beautiful
inside his burial mound,
though dead by violence

and unavenged.
Men said that he was chanting
verses about honour
and that four lights burned

in corners of the chamber:
which opened then, as he turned
with a joyful face
to look at the moon.

North

I returned to a long strand,
the hammered shod of a bay,
and found only the secular
powers of the Atlantic thundering.

I faced the unmagical
invitations of Iceland,
the pathetic colonies
of Greenland, and suddenly

those fabulous raiders,
those lying in Orkney and Dublin
measured against
their long swords rusting,

those in the solid
belly of stone ships,
those hacked and glinting
in the gravel of thawed streams

were ocean-deafened voices
warning me, lifted again
in violence and epiphany.
The longship's swimming tongue

was buoyant with hindsight –
it said Thor's hammer swung
to geography and trade,
thick-witted couplings and revenges,

the hatreds and behindbacks
of the althing, lies and women,
exhaustions nominated peace,
memory incubating the spilled blood.

It said, 'Lie down
in the word-hoard, burrow
the coil and gleam
of your furrowed brain.

Compose in darkness.
Expect aurora borealis
in the long foray
but no cascade of light.

Keep your eye clear
as the bleb of the icicle,
trust the feel of what nubbed treasure
your hands have known.'

Viking Dublin: Trial Pieces

I

It could be a jaw-bone
or a rib or a portion cut
from something sturdier:
anyhow, a small outline

was incised, a cage
or trellis to conjure in.
Like a child's tongue
following the toils

of his calligraphy,
like an eel swallowed
in a basket of eels,
the line amazes itself,

eluding the hand
that fed it,
a bill in flight,
a swimming nostril.

II

These are trial pieces,
the craft's mystery
improvised on bone:
foliage, bestiaries,

interlacings elaborate
as the netted routes
of ancestry and trade.
That have to be

magnified on display

so that the nostril
is a migrant prow
sniffing the Liffey,

swanning it up to the ford,
dissembling itself
in antler combs, bone pins,
coins, weights, scale-pans.

III

Like a long sword
sheathed in its moisting
burial clays,
the keel stuck fast

in the slip of the bank,
its clinker-built hull
spined and plosive
as *Dublin*.

And now we reach in
for shards of the vertebrae,
the ribs of hurdle,
the mother-wet caches –

and for this trial piece
incised by a child,
a longship, a buoyant
migrant line.

IV

That enters my longhand,
turns cursive, unscarfing
a zoomorphic wake,
a worm of thought

I follow into the mud.
I am Hamlet the Dane,
skull-handler, parablist,
smeller of rot

in the state, infused
with its poisons,
pinioned by ghosts
and affections,

murders and pieties,
coming to consciousness
by jumping in graves,
dithering, blathering.

V

Come fly with me,
come sniff the wind
with the expertise
of the Vikings –

neighbourly, scoretaking
killers, haggers
and hagglers, gombeen-men,
hoarders of grudges and gain.

With a butcher's aplomb
they spread out your lungs
and made you warm wings
for your shoulders.

Old fathers, be with us.
Old cunning assessors
of feuds and of sites
for ambush or town.

VI

'Did you ever hear tell,'
said Jimmy Farrell,
'of the skulls they have
in the city of Dublin?

White skulls and black skulls
and yellow skulls, and some
with full teeth, and some
haven't only but one,'

and compounded history
in the pan of 'an old Dane,
maybe, was drowned
in the Flood.'

My words lick around
cobbled quays, go hunting
lightly as pampooties
over the skull-capped ground.

The Digging Skeleton

After Baudelaire

I

You find anatomical plates
Buried along these dusty quays
Among books yellowed like mummies
Slumbering in forgotten crates,

Drawings touched with an odd beauty
As if the illustrator had
Responded gravely to the sad
Mementoes of anatomy –

Mysterious candid studies
Of red slobland around the bones.
Like this one: flayed men and skeletons
Digging the earth like navvies.

II

Sad gang of apparitions,
Your skinned muscles like plaited sedge
And your spines hooped towards the sunk edge
Of the spade, my patient ones,

Tell me, as you labour hard
To break this unrelenting soil,
What barns are there for you to fill?
What farmer dragged you from the boneyard?

Or are you emblems of the truth,
Death's lifers, hauled from the narrow cell
And stripped of night-shirt shrouds, to tell:
'This is the reward of faith

In rest eternal. Even death
Lies. The void deceives.
We do not fall like autumn leaves
To sleep in peace. Some traitor breath

Revives our clay, sends us abroad
And by the sweat of our stripped brows
We earn our deaths; our one repose
When the bleeding instep finds its spade.'

Bone Dreams

I

White bone found
on the grazing:
the rough, porous
language of touch

and its yellowing, ribbed
impression in the grass –
a small ship-burial.
As dead as stone,

flint-find, nugget
of chalk,
I touch it again,
I wind it in

the sling of mind
to pitch it at England
and follow its drop
to strange fields.

II

Bone-house:
a skeleton
in the tongue's
old dungeons.

I push back
through dictions,
Elizabethan canopies.
Norman devices,

the erotic mayflowers

of Provence
and the ivied Latins
of churchmen

to the scop's
twang, the iron
flash of consonants
cleaving the line.

III

In the coffered
riches of grammar
and declensions
I found *ban hus*,

its fire, benches,
wattle and rafters,
where the soul
fluttered a while

in the roofspace.
There was a small crock
for the brain,
and a cauldron

of generation
swung at the centre:
love-den, blood-holt,
dream-bower.

IV

Come back past
philology and kennings,
re-enter memory
where the bone's lair

is a love-nest
in the grass.
I hold my lady's head
like a crystal

and ossify myself
by gazing: I am screes
on her escarpments,
a chalk giant

carved upon her downs.
Soon my hands, on the sunken
fosse of her spine
move towards the passes.

V

And we end up
cradling each other
between the lips
of an earthwork.

As I estimate
for pleasure
her knuckles' paving,
the turning stiles

of the elbows,
the vallum of her brow
and the long wicket
of collar-bone,

I have begun to pace
the Hadrian's Wall
of her shoulder, dreaming
of Maiden Castle.

VI

One morning in Devon
I found a dead mole
with the dew still beading it.
I had thought the mole

a big-boned coulter
but there it was,
small and cold
as the thick of a chisel.

I was told, 'Blow,
blow back the fur on his head.
Those little points
were the eyes.

And feel the shoulders.'
I touched small distant Pennines,
a pelt of grass and grain
running south.

Come to the Bower

My hands come, touched
By sweetbriar and tangled vetch,
Foraging past the burst gizzards
Of coin-hoards

To where the dark-bowered queen,
Whom I unpin,
Is waiting. Out of the black maw
Of the peat, sharpened willow

Withdraws gently.
I unwrap skins and see
The pot of the skull,
The damp tuck of each curl

Reddish as a fox's brush,
A mark of a gorget in the flesh
Of her throat. And spring water
Starts to rise around her.

I reach past
The riverbed's washed
Dream of gold to the bullion
Of her Venus bone.

Bog Queen

I lay waiting
between turf-face and demesne wall,
between heathery levels
and glass-toothed stone.

My body was braille
for the creeping influences:
dawn suns groped over my head
and cooled at my feet,

through my fabrics and skins
the seeps of winter
digested me,
the illiterate roots

pondered and died
in the cavings
of stomach and socket.
I lay waiting

on the gravel bottom,
my brain darkening,
a jar of spawn
fermenting underground

dreams of Baltic amber.
Bruised berries under my nails,
the vital hoard reducing
in the crock of the pelvis.

My diadem grew carious,
gemstones dropped
in the peat floe
like the bearings of history.

My sash was a black glacier
wrinkling, dyed weaves
and phoenician stitchwork
retted on my breasts'

soft moraines.
I knew winter cold
like the nuzzle of fjords
at my thighs –

the soaked fledge, the heavy
swaddle of hides.
My skull hibernated
in the wet nest of my hair.

Which they robbed.
I was barbered
and stripped
by a turfcutter's spade

who veiled me again
and packed coomb softly
between the stone jambs
at my head and my feet.

Till a peer's wife bribed him.
The plait of my hair,
a slimy birth-cord
of bog, had been cut

and I rose from the dark,
hacked bone, skull-ware,
frayed stitches, tufts,
small gleams on the bank.

The Grauballe Man

As if he had been poured
in tar, he lies
on a pillow of turf
and seems to weep

the black river of himself.
The grain of his wrists
is like bog oak,
the ball of his heel

like a basalt egg.
His instep has shrunk
cold as a swan's foot
or a wet swamp root.

His hips are the ridge
and purse of a mussel,
his spine an eel arrested
under a glisten of mud.

The head lifts,
the chin is a visor
raised above the vent
of his slashed throat

that has tanned and toughened.
The cured wound
opens inwards to a dark
elderberry place.

Who will say 'corpse'
to his vivid cast?
Who will say 'body'
to his opaque repose?

And his rusted hair,
a mat unlikely
as a foetus's.
I first saw his twisted face

in a photograph,
a head and shoulder
out of the peat,
bruised like a forceps baby,

but now he lies
perfected in my memory,
down to the red horn
of his nails,

hung in the scales
with beauty and atrocity:
with the Dying Gaul
too strictly compassed

on his shield,
with the actual weight
of each hooded victim,
slashed and dumped.

Punishment

I can feel the tug
of the halter at the nape
of her neck, the wind
on her naked front.

It blows her nipples
to amber beads,
it shakes the frail rigging
of her ribs.

I can see her drowned
body in the bog,
the weighing stone,
the floating rods and boughs.

Under which at first
she was a barked sapling
that is dug up
oak-bone, brain-firkin:

her shaved head
like a stubble of black corn,
her blindfold a soiled bandage,
her noose a ring

to store
the memories of love.
Little adulteress,
before they punished you

you were flaxen-haired,
undernourished, and your
tar-black face was beautiful.
My poor scapegoat,

I almost love you
but would have cast, I know,
the stones of silence.
I am the artful voyeur

of your brain's exposed
and darkened combs,
your muscles' webbing
and all your numbered bones:

I who have stood dumb
when your betraying sisters,
cauled in tar,
wept by the railings,

who would connive
in civilized outrage
yet understand the exact
and tribal, intimate revenge.

Strange Fruit

Here is the girl's head like an exhumed gourd.
Oval-faced, prune-skinned, prune-stones for teeth.
They unswaddled the wet fern of her hair
And made an exhibition of its coil,
Let the air at her leathery beauty.
Pash of tallow, perishable treasure:
Her broken nose is dark as a turf clod,
Her eyeholes blank as pools in the old workings.
Diodorus Siculus confessed
His gradual ease among the likes of this:
Murdered, forgotten, nameless, terrible
Beheaded girl, outstaring axe
And beatification, outstaring
What had begun to feel like reverence.

Kinship

I

Kinned by hieroglyphic
peat on a spreadfield
to the strangled victim,
the love-nest in the bracken,

I step through origins
like a dog turning
its memories of wilderness
on the kitchen mat:

the bog floor shakes,
water cheeps and lisps
as I walk down
rushes and heather.

I love this turf-face,
its black incisions,
the cooped secrets
of process and ritual;

I love the spring
off the ground,
each bank a gallows drop,
each open pool

the unstopped mouth
of an urn, a moon-drinker,
not to be sounded
by the naked eye.

II

Quagmire, swampland, morass:

the slime kingdoms,
domains of the cold-blooded,
of mud pads and dirtied eggs.

But *bog*
meaning soft,
the fall of windless rain,
pupil of amber.

Ruminant ground,
digestion of mollusc
and seed-pod,
deep pollen-bin.

Earth-pantry, bone-vault,
sun-bank, embalmer
of votive goods
and sabred fugitives.

Insatiable bride.
Sword-swallower,
casket, midden,
floe of history.

Ground that will strip
its dark side,
nesting ground,
outback of my mind.

III

I found a turf-spade
hidden under bracken,
laid flat, and overgrown
with a green fog.

As I raised it
the soft lips of the growth

muttered and split,
a tawny rut

opening at my feet
like a shed skin,
the shaft wettish
as I sank it upright

and beginning to
steam in the sun.
And now they have twinned
that obelisk:

among the stones,
under a bearded cairn
a love-nest is disturbed,
catkin and bog-cotton tremble

as they raise up
the cloven oak-limb:
I stand at the edge of centuries
facing a goddess.

IV

This centre holds
and spreads,
sump and seedbed,
a bag of waters

and a melting grave.
The mothers of autumn
sour and sink,
ferments of husk and leaf

deepen their ochres.
Mosses come to a head,
heather unseeds,

brackens deposit

their bronze.
This is the vowel of earth
dreaming its root
in flowers and snow,

mutation of weathers
and seasons,
a windfall composing
the floor it rots into.

I grew out of all this
like a weeping willow
inclined to
the appetites of gravity.

V

The hand-carved felloes
of the turf-cart wheels
buried in a litter
of turf mould,

the cupid's bow
of the tail-board,
the socketed lips
of the cribs:

I deified the man
who rode there,
god of the waggon,
the hearth-feeder.

I was his privileged
attendant, a bearer
of bread and drink,
the squire of his circuits.

When summer died
and wives forsook the fields
we were abroad,
saluted, given right-of-way.

Watch our progress
down the haw-lit hedges,
my manly pride
when he speaks to me.

VI

And you, Tacitus,
observe how I make my grove
on an old crannog
piled by the fearful dead:

a desolate peace.
Our mother ground
is sour with the blood
of her faithful,

they lie gargling
in her sacred heart
as the legions stare
from the ramparts.

Come back to this
'island of the ocean'
where nothing will suffice.
Read the inhumed faces

of casualty and victim;
report us fairly,
how we slaughter
for the common good

and shave the heads
of the notorious,
how the goddess swallows
our love and terror.

Ocean's Love to Ireland

I

Speaking broad Devonshire,
Ralegh has backed the maid to a tree
As Ireland is backed to England

And drives inland
Till all her strands are breathless:
'Sweesir, Swatter! Sweesir, Swatter!'

He is water, he is ocean, lifting
Her farthingale like a scarf of weed lifting
In the front of a wave.

II

Yet his superb crest inclines to Cynthia
Even while it runs its bent
In the rivers of Lee and Blackwater.

Those are the plashy spots where he would lay
His cape before her. In London, his name
Will rise on water, and on these dark seepings:

Smerwick sowed with the mouthing corpses
Of six hundred papists, 'as gallant and good
Personages as ever were beheld.'

III

The ruined maid complains in Irish,
Ocean has scattered her dreams of fleets,
The Spanish prince has spilled his gold

And failed her. Iambic drums

Of English beat the woods where her poets
Sink like Onan. Rush-light, mushroom-flesh,

She fades from their somnolent clasp
Into ringlet-breath and dew,
The ground possessed and repossessed.

Aisling

He courted her
With a decadent sweet art
Like the wind's vowel
Blowing through the hazels:

'Are you Diana...?'
And was he Actaeon,
His high lament
The stag's exhausted belling?

Act of Union

To-night, a first movement, a pulse,
As if the rain in bogland gathered head
To slip and flood: a bog-burst,
A gash breaking open the ferny bed.
Your back is a firm line of eastern coast
And arms and legs are thrown
Beyond your gradual hills. I caress
The heaving province where our past has grown.
I am the tall kingdom over your shoulder
That you would neither cajole nor ignore.
Conquest is a lie. I grow older
Conceding your half-independent shore
Within whose borders now my legacy
Culminates inexorably.

II

And I am still imperially
Male, leaving you with the pain,
The rending process in the colony,
The battering ram, the boom burst from within.
The act sprouted an obstinate fifth column
Whose stance is growing unilateral.
His heart beneath your heart is a wardrum
Mustering force. His parasitical
And ignorant little fists already
Beat at your borders and I know they're cocked
At me across the water. No treaty
I foresee will salve completely your tracked
And stretchmarked body, the big pain
That leaves you raw, like opened ground, again.

The Betrothal of Cavehill

Gunfire barks its questions off Cavehill
And the profiled basalt maintains its stare
South: proud, protestant and northern, and male.
Adam untouched, before the shock of gender.

They still shoot here for luck over a bridegroom.
The morning I drove out to bed me down
Among my love's hideouts, her pods and broom,
They fired above my car the ritual gun.

Hercules and Antaeus

Sky-born and royal,
snake-choker, dung-heaver,
his mind big with golden apples,
his future hung with trophies,

Hercules has the measure
of resistance and black powers
feeding off the territory.
Antaeus, the mould-hugger,

is weaned at last:
a fall was a renewal
but now he is raised up –
the challenger's intelligence

is a spur of light,
a blue prong graiping him
out of his element
into a dream of loss

and origins – the cradling dark,
the river-veins, the secret gullies
of his strength,
the hatching grounds

of cave and souterrain,
he has bequeathed it all
to elegists. Balor will die
and Byrthnoth and Sitting Bull.

Hercules lifts his arms
in a remorseless V,
his triumph unassailed
by the powers he has shaken,

and lifts and banks Antaeus
high as a profiled ridge,
a sleeping giant,
pap for the dispossessed.

PART II

The Unacknowledged Legislator's Dream

Archimedes thought he could move the world if he could find the right place to position his lever. Billy Hunter said Tarzan shook the world when he jumped down out of a tree.

I sink my crowbar in a chink I know under the masonry of state and statute, I swing on a creeper of secrets into the Bastille. My wronged people cheer from their cages. The guard-dogs are unmuzzled, a soldier pivots a muzzle at the butt of my ear, I am stood blindfolded with my hands above my head until I seem to be swinging from a strappado.

The commandant motions me to be seated. 'I am honoured to add a poet to our list.' He is amused and genuine. 'You'll be safer here, anyhow.'

In the cell, I wedge myself with outstretched arms in the corner and heave, I jump on the concrete flags to test them. Were those your eyes just now at the hatch?

Whatever You Say Say Nothing

I

I'm writing just after an encounter
With an English journalist in search of 'views
On the Irish thing'. I'm back in winter
Quarters where bad news is no longer news,

Where media-men and stringers sniff and point,
Where zoom lenses, recorders and coiled leads
Litter the hotels. The times are out of joint
But I incline as much to rosary beads

As to the jottings and analyses
Of politicians and newspapermen
Who've scribbled down the long campaign from gas
And protest to gelignite and sten,

Who proved upon their pulses 'escalate',
'Backlash' and 'crack down', 'the provisional wing',
'Polarization' and 'long-standing hate'.
Yet I live here, I live here too, I sing,

Expertly civil-tongued with civil neighbours
On the high wires of first wireless reports,
Sucking the fake taste, the stony flavours
Of those sanctioned, old, elaborate retorts:

'Oh, it's disgraceful, surely, I agree.'
'Where's it going to end?' 'It's getting worse.'
'They're murderers.' 'Internment, understandably...'
The 'voice of sanity' is getting hoarse.

II

Men die at hand. In blasted street and home

The gelignite's a common sound effect:
As the man said when Celtic won, 'The Pope of Rome
's a happy man this night.' His flock suspect

In their deepest heart of hearts the heretic
Has come at last to heel and to the stake.
We tremble near the flames but want no truck
With the actual firing. We're on the make

As ever. Long sucking the hind tit,
Cold as a witch's and as hard to swallow,
Still leaves us fork-tongued on the border bit:
The liberal papist note sounds hollow

When amplified and mixed in with the bangs
That shake all hearts and windows day and night.
(It's tempting here to rhyme on 'labour pangs'
And diagnose a rebirth in our plight

But that would be to ignore other symptoms.
Last night you didn't need a stethoscope
To hear the eructation of Orange drums
Allergic equally to Pearse and Pope.)

On all sides 'little platoons' are mustering –
The phrase is Cruise O'Brien's via that great
Backlash, Burke – while I sit here with a pestering
Drouth for words at once both gaff and bait

To lure the tribal shoals to epigram
And order. I believe any of us
Could draw the line through bigotry and sham,
Given the right line, *aere perennius*.

III

'Religion's never mentioned here,' of course.
'You know them by their eyes,' and hold your tongue.

'One side's as bad as the other,' never worse.
Christ, it's near time that some small leak was sprung

In the great dykes the Dutchman made
To dam the dangerous tide that followed Seamus.
Yet for all this art and sedentary trade
I am incapable. The famous

Northern reticence, the tight gag of place
And times: yes, yes. Of the 'wee six' I sing
Where to be saved you only must save face
And whatever you say, you say nothing.

Smoke-signals are loud-mouthed compared with us:
Manoeuvrings to find out name and school,
Subtle discrimination by addresses
With hardly an exception to the rule

That Norman, Ken and Sidney signalled Prod,
And Seamus (call me Sean) was sure-fire Pape.
Oh, land of password, handgrip, wink and nod,
Of open minds as open as a trap,

Where tongues lie coiled, as under flames lie wicks,
Where half of us, as in a wooden horse
Were cabin'd and confined like wily Greeks,
Besieged within the siege, whispering morse.

IV

This morning from a dewy motorway
I saw the new camp for the internees:
A bomb had left a crater of fresh clay
In the roadside, and over in the trees

Machine-gun posts defined a real stockade.
There was that white mist you get on a low ground
And it was déjà-vu, some film made

Of Stalag 17, a bad dream with no sound.

Is there a life before death? That's chalked up
In Ballymurphy. Competence with pain,
Coherent miseries, a bite and sup:
We hug our little destiny again.

Freedman

Indeed, slavery comes nearest to its justification in the early Roman Empire: for a man from a 'backward' race might be brought within the pale of civilization, educated and trained in a craft or a profession, and turned into a useful member of society.
  R. H. BARROW: THE ROMANS

Subjugated yearly under arches,
Manumitted by parchments and degrees,
My murex was the purple dye of lents
On calendars all fast and abstinence.

'*Memento homo quia pulvis es.*'
I would kneel to be impressed by ashes,
A silk friction, a light stipple of dust –
I was under the thumb too like all my caste.

One of the earth-starred denizens, indelibly,
I sought the mark in vain on the groomed optimi:
Their estimating, census-taking eyes
Fastened on my mouldy brow like lampreys.

Then poetry arrived in that city –
I would abjure all cant and self-pity –
And poetry wiped my brow and sped me.
Now they will say I bite the hand that fed me.

Singing School

Fair seedtime had my soul, and I grew up
Fostered alike by beauty and by fear;
Much favoured in my birthplace, and no less
In that beloved Vale to which, erelong,
I was transplanted...
    WILLIAM WORDSWORTH: THE PRELUDE

He [the stable-boy] had a book of Orange rhymes, and the days
when we read them together in the hay-loft gave me the pleasure
of rhyme for the first time. Later on I can remember being told,
when there was a rumour of a Fenian rising, that rifles were
being handed out to the Orangemen: and presently, when I began
to dream of my future life, I thought I would like to die fighting
the Fenians.
    W. B. YEATS: AUTOBIOGRAPHIES

1. The Ministry of Fear
For Seamus Deane

Well, as Kavanagh said, we have lived
In important places. The lonely scarp
Of St Columb's College, where I billeted
For six years, overlooked your Bogside.
I gazed into new worlds: the inflamed throat
Of Brandywell, its floodlit dogtrack,
The throttle of the hare. In the first week
I was so homesick I couldn't even eat
The biscuits left to sweeten my exile.
I threw them over the fence one night
In September 1951
When the lights of houses in the Lecky Road
Were amber in the fog. It was an act
Of stealth.
            Then Belfast, and then Berkeley.
Here's two on's are sophisticated,
Dabbling in verses till they have become
A life: from bulky envelopes arriving
In vacation time to slim volumes
Despatched 'with the author's compliments'.
Those poems in longhand, ripped from the wire spine
Of your exercise-book, bewildered me –
Vowels and ideas bandied free
As the seed-pots blowing off our sycamores.
I tried to write about the sycamores
And innovated a South Derry rhyme
With *hushed* and *lulled* full chimes for *pushed* and *pulled*.
Those hobnailed boots from beyond the mountain
Were walking, by God, all over the fine
Lawns of elocution.
                     Have our accents
Changed? 'Catholics, in general, don't speak
As well as students from the Protestant schools.'
Remember that stuff? Inferiority

Complexes, stuff that dreams were made on.

'What's your name, Heaney?'
                                              'Heaney, Father.'
                                                                          'Fair
Enough.'
                  On my first day, the leather strap
Went epileptic in the Big Study,
Its echoes plashing over our bowed heads,
But I still wrote home that a boarder's life
Was not so bad, shying as usual.

On long vacations, then, I came to life
In the kissing seat of an Austin Sixteen
Parked at a gable, the engine running,
My fingers tight as ivy on her shoulders,
A light left burning for her in the kitchen.
And heading back for home, the summer's
Freedom dwindling night by night, the air
All moonlight and a scent of hay, policemen
Swung their crimson flashlamps, crowding round
The car like black cattle, snuffing and pointing
The muzzle of a sten-gun in my eye:
'What's your name, driver?'
                                            'Seamus...'
                                                          Seamus?

They once read my letters at a roadblock
And shone their torches on your hieroglyphics,
'Svelte dictions' in a very florid hand.

Ulster was British, but with no rights on
The English lyric: all around us, though
We hadn't named it, the ministry of fear.

2. A Constable Calls

His bicycle stood at the window-sill,
The rubber cowl of a mud-splasher
Skirting the front mudguard,
Its fat black handlegrips

Heating in sunlight, the 'spud'
Of the dynamo gleaming and cocked back,
The pedal treads hanging relieved
Of the boot of the law.

His cap was upside down
On the floor, next his chair.
The line of its pressure ran like a bevel
In his slightly sweating hair.

He had unstrapped
The heavy ledger, and my father
Was making tillage returns
In acres, roods, and perches.

Arithmetic and fear.
I sat staring at the polished holster
With its buttoned flap, the braid cord
Looped into the revolver butt.

'Any other root crops?
Mangolds? Marrowstems? Anything like that?'
'No.' But was there not a line
Of turnips where the seed ran out

In the potato field? I assumed
Small guilts and sat
Imagining the black hole in the barracks.
He stood up, shifted the baton-case

Further round on his belt,
Closed the domesday book,
Fitted his cap back with two hands,
And looked at me as he said goodbye.

A shadow bobbed in the window.
He was snapping the carrier spring
Over the ledger. His boot pushed off
And the bicycle ticked, ticked, ticked.

3. Orange Drums, Tyrone, 1966

The lambeg balloons at his belly, weighs
Him back on his haunches, lodging thunder
Grossly there between his chin and his knees.
He is raised up by what he buckles under.

Each arm extended by a seasoned rod,
He parades behind it. And though the drummers
Are granted passage through the nodding crowd,
It is the drums preside, like giant tumours.

To every cocked ear, expert in its greed,
His battered signature subscribes 'No Pope'.
The goatskin's sometimes plastered with his blood.
The air is pounding like a stethoscope.

4. Summer 1969

While the Constabulary covered the mob
Firing into the Falls, I was suffering
Only the bullying sun of Madrid.
Each afternoon, in the casserole heat
Of the flat, as I sweated my way through
The life of Joyce, stinks from the fishmarket
Rose like the reek off a flax-dam.
At night on the balcony, gules of wine,
A sense of children in their dark corners,
Old women in black shawls near open windows,
The air a canyon rivering in Spanish.
We talked our way home over starlit plains
Where patent leather of the Guardia Civil
Gleamed like fish-bellies in flax-poisoned waters.

'Go back,' one said, 'try to touch the people.'
Another conjured Lorca from his hill.
We sat through death-counts and bullfight reports
On the television, celebrities
Arrived from where the real thing still happened.

I retreated to the cool of the Prado.
Goya's 'Shootings of the Third of May'
Covered a wall – the thrown-up arms
And spasm of the rebel, the helmeted
And knapsacked military, the efficient
Rake of the fusillade. In the next room,
His nightmares, grafted to the palace wall –
Dark cyclones, hosting, breaking; Saturn
Jewelled in the blood of his own children;
Gigantic Chaos turning his brute hips
Over the world. Also, that holmgang
Where two berserks club each other to death
For honour's sake, greaved in a bog, and sinking.

He painted with his fists and elbows, flourished
The stained cape of his heart as history charged.

333

5. Fosterage

For Michael McLaverty

'Description is revelation!' Royal
Avenue, Belfast, 1962,
A Saturday afternoon, glad to meet
Me, newly cubbed in language, he gripped
My elbow. 'Listen. Go your own way.
Do your own work. Remember
Katherine Mansfield – *I will tell*
How the laundry basket squeaked... that note of exile.'
But to hell with overstating it:
'Don't have the veins bulging in your biro.'
And then, 'Poor Hopkins!' I have the *Journals*
He gave me, underlined, his buckled self
Obeisant to their pain. He discerned
The lineaments of patience everywhere
And fostered me and sent me out, with words
Imposing on my tongue like obols.

6. Exposure

It is December in Wicklow:
Alders dripping, birches
Inheriting the last light,
The ash tree cold to look at.

A comet that was lost
Should be visible at sunset,
Those million tons of light
Like a glimmer of haws and rose-hips,

And I sometimes see a falling star.
If I could come on meteorite!
Instead I walk through damp leaves,
Husks, the spent flukes of autumn,

Imagining a hero
On some muddy compound,
His gift like a slingstone
Whirled for the desperate.

How did I end up like this?
I often think of my friends'
Beautiful prismatic counselling
And the anvil brains of some who hate me

As I sit weighing and weighing
My responsible *tristia*.
For what? For the ear? For the people?
For what is said behind-backs?

Rain comes down through the alders,
Its low conducive voices
Mutter about let-downs and erosions
And yet each drop recalls

The diamond absolutes.
I am neither internee nor informer;
An inner émigré, grown long-haired
And thoughtful; a wood-kerne

Escaped from the massacre,
Taking protective colouring
From bole and bark, feeling
Every wind that blows;

Who, blowing up these sparks
For their meagre heat, have missed
The once-in-a-lifetime portent,
The comet's pulsing rose.